AMBARI !

R. FORBES-WATSON

AMBARI!

Illustrated by
KIDDELL-MONROE

ROY PUBLISHERS, INC. – NEW YORK

Library of Congress Catalog Card Number 63-16202

Printed in Great Britain by Richard Clay and Company, Ltd.,
Bungay, Suffolk

TO
WEBSTER AND EUAN
FROM
JOAN AND FORBO

CONTENTS

CONTENTS

I

Ali and Juma at Home

IT was pitch dark in the hut. Ali was dreaming
that he was fighting with that bully Squidface.
He was on his back in the dust, and Squidface was
heavy on his chest. Suddenly Ali felt a great strength
filling every muscle in his body. Squidface had no
more strength than a hen compared with him. Fear
showed in Squidface's eyes. Ali filled his lungs for a
great shout of triumph when his ears were deafened.

'COCK-A-DOO-DA-LOOOOO!' rang through Ali's
brain, and he was wide awake, with Joogoo, the
family cock, standing on his chest and telling the world
that there was a new African dawn all ready outside
this darkness.

Ali sat up on his blanket on the floor of the hut,

and Joogoo gave a squawk and flopped on to the ground. Joogoo bumped into a kuku (one of his hens), who screeched and flapped. At once the darkness was filled with screeching, flapping fowls; then Mbwa, the family dog, started to yap.

' A noise of what kind of a sort? ' The shout came from the bed in the corner where Ali's father slept.

' It is the noise of Joogoo and all the kukus and Mbwa, Baba,' said Ali.

' Do you think that I have no ears to tell me that for myself? ' asked Baba. Ali was too polite to say to his father, ' Then why did you ask what kind of a sort it was? '

Then Ali's mother's soft, sleepy voice said, ' Open the door, Ali, and let the kukus out and get some goat's milk.'

' Good, then,' said Ali.

Now that his eyes were used to the darkness, he could see a faint grey line where the light was coming through a crack in the door. He felt about until his fingers touched a piece of thick wire that ran through a hole in the door and curved round the door-post. The two ends were hooked round each other. Ali unfastened the ends and pushed the door, which opened creakily. The first one out was Mbwa, a little yellow dog with a sharp terrier face and a tail curving gaily over his back. Next came Joogoo, long-legged and stately, his comb still scarlet with indignation at all the fuss and bother.

Joogoo clucked commandingly to his hens, and they

2

fussed out after him—all except a grey hen, who
suddenly got it into her head that Ali was going to do
something nasty to her. She started screaming and
flapping, then, terrified at her own commotion, she
flew up to a string tied across the room from one wall
to another, and from which hung a brightly coloured
cloth; this cloth was a curtain behind which Baba
and Mama slept.

' Get out, you! ' cried Ali, and waved his arm at the
hen, swaying and clucking on the string.

With another screech, the hen lost her balance and
disappeared. More shouts from Baba and screams
from the hen, who at last shot from under the curtain
and rushed straight out of the door. Laughter came
from Mama.

' Ee-eh you Mahomed, it is nothing; a kuku, that's
all.'

' A kuku is indeed nothing, Miriamu, yet it can wake
a family from sleep. I perceive hunger; get up now
and cook some food.'

Ali stood just outside the door. He stretched and
filled his lungs with the morning breeze, fresh and
sweet from the Indian Ocean after the smoke, food,
people and hen-smells of his home.

Ali always loved this first moment outside each
morning. First he looked up at the sky. Herds of
clouds were moving slowly from the vast ocean into
the huge land of Africa. Already some of these
clouds were pinky-white where the sun, still out of
sight from Ali, was lighting up their under-sides.

3

The same steady breeze which was driving the clouds brought a roaring noise from the sea: the noise of waves ceaselessly pounding on the coral reef. Beside this sea-noise the wind was making a nearer, gentler land-noise.

All round Ali's home were palm-trees, growing in lines and lines between the shore and the coast-road not far from his house. Ali could see quite a long way through their thin, slightly bent trunks, and these trunks were like the pillars of some huge airy building, pillars holding up a roof of swaying green. The wind swayed this roof, and a pleasant rattling of thousands of leaves mixed with the deep roar from the reef.

Ali then looked around the open space in front of his home. Short creeping grass made a lawn-like place of it. In the middle a large mango-tree sent up a thick brown trunk which held up a dense mass of dark-green leaves. Under the tree was a circle of pale-brown, sandy dust. This circle had been made by cattle and goats when they sheltered from the hot sun and by people when they met beneath it in the evenings to talk.

A little beyond the mango-tree ran the red-earth road, and on the other side of the road was a row of square, thatched houses, each with a little veranda. Beyond these houses was a dense mass of trees. Farther round to the right, on this side of the road, Ali could see the school with its corrugated-iron roof. Nearer still, on the edge of the lawn, stood the house where his friend Juma lived, only a stone's throw from Ali's home.

Joogoo had by now climbed on to a stone and, after arching his body back, sent another trumpet-call ringing out into the morning. At once an answering call came from the other cocks in the village, each trying to crow louder than Joogoo.

The door of Juma's house opened suddenly with a scraping noise, and Juma came running out, followed by a flurry of screaming hens and Mbuzi, his goat.

' That cock of yours is a cock of what kind of a sort? ' said Juma. ' Every day he wakes everyone up while it is still dark and we get turned out into the cold.'

' He's a good cock, that's all,' said Ali. ' It's not his fault that he has more strength than all the other cocks in the place and crows the first.'

Ali's mother's voice came from the doorway.

' Hiya, Ali! Where is the goat's milk? Leave off idle words with Juma and bring it—hurry—and you, Juma, ask your mama for some sugar for me; ours is finished.'

Ali went round to the back of the house where there was a little yard. Fishing-nets were hanging on the fence of thin poles and a big basket-work fishing-trap, made of a criss-cross of thin yellow strips of bamboo. In one corner was a little hut. Ali opened the door, and four goats and a little kid came out and stood about in the yard.

Ali went inside the goats' hut and from a nail on

5

the wall took down a round bowl made from a gourd. Soon he had milked the goats and carried the gourd in to Mama at the back door.

Mama was kneeling on the little veranda, and had already lit a small fire between three stones. On the stones was an aluminium saucepan with no handle, and in it was a white porridge, rather like semolina. Mama was stirring the porridge with a smooth stick and singing gently to herself.

Ali looked down on to his mother's head, which was covered with little furrows of curly hair plaited into neat lines which ran from her forehead to the back of her neck. In between the black lines of hair were thin brown lines where the skin of her head showed through the partings.

Juma's voice was heard outside.

' Hodi ! I bring sugar.'

' Karibu,' called Mama. 'That is good. Ali, bring the sugar-cane and the knife.' With two deft strokes Mama cut off two lengths from the thick bamboo-like stick and gave one to each of the boys. ' Eat those until the porridge is ready,' she said.

The white teeth of the boys crunched off pieces of the cane. They chewed away, swallowing the sweet juice and spitting the white fibres on the ground.

By this time the sun was beginning to throw their shadows on to the whitewashed wall of the house. The porridge began to bubble, and Ali realized that time was getting on. ' I must help Baba to catch fish to-day,' he said.

' Me also,' said Juma.

' What about school? ' asked Mama.

' Fishing is a man's work, school is for children, so fishing comes before school,' said Ali.

' That's it,' said Juma with great conviction. ' The time for school is when the tide is wrong for fishing.'

Mama knew this talk by heart, it happened every morning.

' And when the tide is wrong for fishing you like to go to school? ' she asked.

' Maybe,' said Juma. ' But work comes first.'

' Work of what sort? ' asked Mama.

' Herding the goats,' said Ali promptly.

' E-he-hee,' laughed Mama. ' You are indeed fond of work, but when are you going to learn to read and write and obtain brains? You can't learn these things from fish and goats.'

' We will obtain learning after a while,' said Juma loftily. ' When there is nothing else to be done we agree to obtain learning at the school.'

' That's it ! ' said Ali. ' Although it is all a waste of time. It is not necessary to be able to read and write to catch fish. Does a fish swim only into the net of a learned one? '

' Profit of what kind of a sort comes from foolish words like these? ' Baba suddenly appeared from inside. He was wearing a pair of old khaki shorts, and his dark-brown sturdy body filled the doorway. ' Eh? ' he said fiercely, glaring down at the two boys. ' You're like what?—I don't know.' He went on.

'Do you think I pay money to the Government for your school just to perceive folly of this kind? Does the Government build schools just for nothing?'

'That's it!' said Ali cheekily.

Juma hung his head and drew a squiggle in the sand with his big toe. He did not want Ali's Baba to see he was laughing at Ali's cheek. Both boys knew Baba.

There was a long silence. While Baba was working up some more indignation he glared down at the tops of the curly black heads of the two boys, waiting for someone to look frightened. It was too much for Ali, who began to giggle. Then Juma caught the giggles from Ali. Mama's brown shoulders began to shake. Baba saw he had to do something quickly.

'Leave off this affair of fools,' he said, 'and see where the goats have got to. Go!'

The boys ran out of the backyard, jumping about and shouting with laughter.

Mama threw back her head and gasped helplessly. 'These children like what?'

She saw that Baba's eyes also were full of laughter but Baba said roughly, 'Food ready?'

'Yes, ready,' she said and carried the porridge into the front room.

A great noise of shouting and cheering suddenly came from the direction of the houses on the roadside, and Ali and Juma came rushing back.

'The school is closed—the school is closed to-day,' they were singing.

9

'Who says so?' asked Baba.

'Mwalimu, the Teacher,' said Ali. 'A wire has come from the Bwana District Commissioner. It is the order of the Government.'

'For what reason?' asked Mama.

'The daughter of Kingi George has had a son, and the Government has given everyone an opportunity of rejoicing.'

'Then Kingi George has given the order himself,' said Baba; 'for the Government is his servant.'

'So now I can go fishing?' asked Ali.

Baba thought for a moment or two. He didn't want to show how pleased he was. 'What about the goats?' he asked.

Ali's face lost its eagerness and his eyes filled.

Mama said quietly, 'I will herd them. I want to go to the river to wash my clothes, for there will be a dance to-night for our king's daughter's baby, and I want to talk with the other women down by the river about the baby. Also Juma's mother and I will do each other's hair in readiness.'

Baba listened for a while. The sound of the waves on the reef told him that the tide was nearly out.

'Get the things ready,' he said. 'Let's go.'

Juma ran off to his own home.

II

The Fishing

IT did not take long to get the fishing-things ready. A pair of old sandshoes and a few thin sticks were all that were needed for Baba. Ali picked up his own pair of sandals. The soles were made out of an old car tyre and the uppers of two crossed strips of inner tube sewn on to the soles with pieces of string. He lifted a pair of goggles from a nail on the wall. The goggles were also made of a strip of inner tubing; there was a band to fit round the head, into which were fitted two spectacle-glasses, held in place with rubber solution. Ali hung the goggles round his neck. Baba took a piece of white cloth, the size of a table-cloth, and wrapped it over one shoulder. Ali carried a large flat basket, woven of grass. They were ready.

A little path wound away from the back of the house and through the palms, then through some thick, jungly bushes and tall trees. Suddenly it came out on to an open grassy space, past a huge, fat baobab-tree. Ali always ran along the path here, because inside the hollow, grey, swelling trunk lived all sorts of evil spirits. Through a few palm-trees Ali saw the water shining like silver in the lagoon, and now he ran even faster, because he could not wait to reach it. The grassy space ended in a bank, down which Ali jumped. He landed with his feet buried in the loose coral sand of the beach. Juma, racing to catch him up, landed beside him.

The beach sloped steeply down to the water, which was lapping gently on the shining wet sand. Soon Ali was wading out into the lagoon towards Baba's canoe. The canoe was lying in a patch of pale-green water which glowed among patches of every shade of brown where seaweed and coral grew. The canoe floated over an expanse of white sand, and this was what gave the patch its pale green colour.

The canoe was carved out of a tree-trunk, and was finely pointed at both ends. Laid across it were two poles and, from these, other poles slanted down and pierced two pointed planks, which just touched the water on each side and prevented the canoe from toppling over. The canoe bobbed lightly in the little waves and tugged gently at its long grass rope, which could be seen in the clear water stretching in a brown line to a rock on the bottom.

The water was up to Ali's chest when he reached the canoe, but he easily heaved himself up between the stern and the cross-poles and went to the bows to make room for Baba to get in.

Inside, the canoe was surprisingly narrow and deep. There was only just room for one's legs to pass each other when moving from one end to the other, and yet the sides came up above one's knees. There were no seats, but the cross-poles were there to sit on. In the bottom of the canoe water slopped about over Ali's feet. In this water there were two long, thin sticks, nearly the length of the canoe, and an old pineapple-tin. Ali knelt down and began to bale out the water with the tin. Suddenly the canoe gave a great lurch and Baba was aboard.

Baba bent down and picked up one of the long, thin sticks.

' Pull in the rope,' he said.

Ali leant down over the bows and caught the rope near where the end was tied through a hole which pierced the solid wood at the water-line. He pulled, and the rope came up and the canoe moved slowly towards its anchoring rock. With a big heave Ali hoisted up the rock, undid the rope, and the rock splashed back.

Baba, by now, was beginning to pole the canoe along with the stick; although so thin, it was surprisingly strong. And they headed out towards the line of biscuit colour which was the uncovered reef and the dazzling white where the waves were dashing themselves into spray against it. A few yards away Juma and his father were moving off in their long canoe, which, unlike Baba's, had no steadying out-riggers.

Ali seized the other poling-stick and, standing in the bows, helped to pole the canoe along. Out on the reef there were other canoes here and there and black specks where other men and boys were fishing. In one place were some pink specks, white people on holiday who had waded and swum out to the reef to explore. In the water between Ali and the reef was a bright yellow thing being dragged along by two white boys, who were struggling with it to the reef.

As the canoe glided nearer to the reef the noise of the sea, a continuous shuddering roar, grew louder and louder. Soon the canoe bumped gently against a rocky shelf. Ali jumped out with the rope, found a lump of coral under the surface, and tied the canoe so that it floated clear of the shelf. Juma and his father moored their canoe close by.

Baba got out and began to wade slowly through the shallow water, the thin sticks in his hand. Every now and then he stooped down and poked with his sticks under rocks and into crevices. Suddenly his hand shot down like a flash into the water and came up again with a greyish shape in it. Round his forearm were coiled things like young snakes, writhing and twisting.

Just then the two white boys came up, towing their yellow rubber dinghy behind them. They went to see what Baba had caught.

'Jambo!' they said. 'This is a thing of what sort?'

'Jambo Sirs,' smiled Baba; he was always glad when white people spoke to him in his own language. 'This is called Pweza, the squid.'

'Gosh! Isn't it ugly!' said one of the boys, as Baba opened his hand to show the squid's fat body with its evil eyes. 'Its eyes are in its body, it seems to have no mouth, and look at that horrid-looking tube sticking out.'

'I think that is its jet for squirting water out to make it shoot along,' said the other boy. 'Its mouth is where?' he asked Baba in his language.

Baba brushed the clinging tentacles off his arm with his other hand and flicked his wrist so that the writhing 'snakes' hung down. He made a quick movement with his fingers in among the 'roots' of the tentacles and pulled the squid inside out! 'Now he is dead,' said Baba, and showed the two boys a beak-like thing where the mouth of the squid had been hidden by the tentacles.

Even now the arms of the squid were feeling about, and Baba held one out near the arm of one of the white boys. All along the underside of the tentacle were rows of little cup-shaped suckers of papery thinness which were fastened to the tentacle by short stalks. As soon as one of the little suckers touched the boy's arm it stuck on with a gentle yet firm grip. Then other suckers softly clung until they were all fastened on.

' Ugh! It's horrid; try it, Peter,' said the boy, unpeeling the tentacle from his arm and rubbing himself to get rid of the tickling feeling it left.

' Yes, it feels sticky, and yet isn't,' said the other boy after he had tried it. ' Imagine if it was a big octopus.' He turned to Baba. ' Are there pweza like this, only very big? ' he asked.

' Oh, yes,' said Baba, ' in the deep water. They can catch a man if he comes too close to one.'

' Do-o they ever come in here? ' said Peter, pointing to the lagoon.

' No, Sir,' laughed Baba, ' they don't like shallow water. You can't be caught in there.'

While this talk was going on, Ali had been standing close by, looking at the two white boys. He had often seen white boys before on the beach, but he never got over their strangeness. These two were about his own size. They seemed not so strong as he in the body, and yet he wasn't so sure. There was

something about the way they looked and held themselves that seemed to give them strength. They must
know much more than he did, and yet they were
ignorant of squids and lots of things that he knew.
How pink their skin was!—and thin compared with
his thick brown skin. They had little golden hairs all
over their arms and legs. Juma had no hairs on his
body at all. Then there was their bright-yellow
dinghy, which hardly touched the water it was so
light. Ali glanced at it again, gave a cry, and dashed
off. The dinghy was being blown away into the
lagoon.

' You ass, Andrew,' shouted Peter. ' You let go the
string.'

' Come on,' yelled Andrew. ' Oh—that chap has
got it. Well done,' he said to Ali, who was dragging
the dinghy back, all his white teeth flashing as he
laughed.

' You have brought this thing here for why? ' Ali
asked Andrew and Peter as he handed them back the
towing string.

' We want to find those beautiful things that live in
the water, I don't know what you call them,' said
Peter. 'What are "shells " in Swahili, Andrew? ' he
asked.

' Don't know,' said Andrew, but he looked down
into the water and soon held up a small shell. ' Like
this,' he said to Ali, ' only big and *maridadi*.'

' Now I understand,' said Ali. ' I have come to
get some to sell to the white people in the hoteli.'

He pointed to the white buildings half-hidden in the trees on the beach of the lagoon.

' That is our hotel,' said Andrew. ' We can't find any of the whatsits we want, the *maridadi* ones.'

' I tell you what,' said Peter. ' You help us to find these *nini hiis* and then we can put all we find into our—er—canoe. It will hold more than your basket, and then we can sail across with them to the hotel.'

' Yes,' said Andrew. ' And if you let us have one *nini hii* we will ask our Mama to buy four or five.'

' Good,' said Ali.

He liked these boys, they knew how to make a bargain. Just then Juma came up and was added to the party.

They had all forgotten about the roar of the breakers, because their ears and voices were used to it, but then a thin voice was heard piercing the noise. It was Baba, now some way off, shouting to Ali. Andrew and Peter could not make out a word, but Ali kept on answering :

' Eh !—Eh ! ' and looked pleased.

' What does your Baba say? ' asked Peter.

' He says that this evening, when the water is low like this again, everyone is going to drive the fish up there.' Ali pointed to the rocky headland a mile or two up the lagoon which jutted out as far as the reef. ' Then we will catch many fish to eat at the big dance to-night when we rejoice over the son of the daughter of Kingi George.'

' It must be good to catch fish like that,' said Andrew.

'It is good completely,' laughed Juma and Ali.

The two African boys led the way off the reef into the deeper water along the wall that the reef made. The wall had been eaten away underneath into little caves. When they came to deeper water Ali slipped his goggles up from round his neck over his eyes and, holding his breath, put his head under water. Then he dived down and came up again with a big shell which he dumped into the dinghy.

'That's the kind we want,' said Peter.

The shell was as long as his forearm and had five large spikes curving out all along one side. Below the spikes there was a shiny, smooth, purplish part that disappeared into a large opening into which the creature which had made the shell had now withdrawn. On the other side of the opening was an even more beautiful shining pink expanse, as smooth as the smoothest china. On top the shell was wrinkled in waves up to where it started to curve towards the curving spikes.

'How do we get the dudu out that lives inside?' asked Andrew.

'I will get it out for you and bring its house to you to-morrow,' said Ali. 'It has to be put in boiling water, and then the dudu can be pulled out with a piece of wire.'

'Good,' said Peter. 'But first our Mama must see it.'

'That's it,' said Ali.

Then Andrew and Peter took turns to wear Ali's

goggles. A fascinating world came into view as soon as their eyes were below the surface of the water. They could see so clearly that they almost forgot that they were under water and found it hard to remember to hold their breath. Corals with branches, starfish, crabs, shells, all sprang into view. Ripples of light, flashed down to the bottom by the ripples on the surface, played over all. Now and then, tiny fish, the size of bees or moths, swam cheekily up to within a few inches of their eyes and then flicked away. All along the wall of the reef were other brightly coloured fish nibbling at the coral. The boys stayed down for so long each time that they came up gasping for air.

So the morning passed, until the dinghy had a good cargo of shells for Ali and Juma to sell. Andrew and Peter had collected a complete coral standing on a rock. The water was getting deeper as the tide began to sweep once more over the reef. The four boys climbed into the dinghy, and Peter stood up in the stern. He acted as a mast and held the mackintosh apron up for a sail. The wind caught this sail, and the dinghy was soon crabbing its way at a good speed towards the dazzling white beach.

Peter and Andrew's mother was waiting for them when they landed and, after admiring the shells, she ordered three each from Ali and Juma. The two white boys gave Ali and Juma a slab of chocolate apiece and told them not to bring back the shells until four days had passed, as they would be away on a journey along the coast to Lamu.

The Fishing

Ali and Juma set off together with the heavy basket of shells along the beach towards their homes. Ali could see his Baba coming in in his canoe. Baba had fixed the two punting-sticks upright in the bows and fastened to them the piece of cloth for a sail. The canoe was gliding along so fast that Ali had to run to be at the patch of sand where the canoe was moored in time to meet it and tie the grass rope once more to the rock.

Baba had caught enough squids for the family, and Ali had his slab of chocolate and enough shells to sell for many shillings.

This evening there was to be a big fishing, and to-night the whole village would dance.

III

Lost at Sea

THAT evening, as the sun was beginning to
shine into their front door, Baba and Ali went
out again to the canoe. Juma and his father
went with them, and soon they were heading in
their two canoes up the lagoon past the hotel. In
front and behind them were other canoes, all
making for the place where the big fishing was to
begin.

Some distance past the hotel, a stream flowed out
into the lagoon from a clump of big trees. Opposite
the mouth of the stream there was an opening in the
reef where the fresh water had prevented the little
creatures that build up coral reefs from filling in the
gap. The river water was a muddy red, and was
flowing swiftly.

' Rain has fallen in the hills,' said Baba, and he and
Ali bent to their punting-sticks to send the canoe
across the stream quickly before it could be swept
along with it.

The bottom was out of reach of their sticks, but they

easily shot across into the clear shallow sea-water on the other side.

Quite a fleet of canoes had formed up in a straggling line right across the lagoon from the beach to the reef. Each canoe was full of the black bodies of men and boys. The sound of shouting and singing came clearly across the water, mingled with the beating of sticks on the sides of the canoes and the splashing of sticks in the water.

Slowly the line of canoes moved forward towards the rocky headland which jutted out and closed the lagoon. Out of sight, under the shining water, the fish were hurrying away from the noise and splashes. Where the lagoon was very shallow, boys jumped out of their fathers' canoes and splashed alongside, laughing and shouting, throwing water at each other, coming to grips and ducking each other, until shouts from their fathers reminded them that they must keep up with the canoes and fill in the gaps between them properly.

At last, when they were near the headland, splashes could be seen on the surface of the water ahead, where big fish were chasing the crowded little fish and driving them up until they shot for a moment along the top of the water. This was the sign for the line of canoes to stop. The men climbed out of their boats with nets over their arms, leaving the boys to look after the canoes. Ali and Juma each followed his own father, towing his canoe behind him.

Baba and Juma's father were holding a net between

23

them and wading forward together. Every now and then their keen eyes would see a shoal of fish. Carefully, they would surround the shoal with the net. The fish, terrified, darted in every direction, and the twitching of the net would show that several had dashed into it and were struggling in the meshes. Baba and Juma's father would each draw in his end of the net in folds, every now and then reaching down to pick out a fish and thread it through its mouth and gills on to a string tied to their waists. When there were enough on the string the fish were taken off it and put in the canoes.

When the line of fishermen reached the end of the lagoon everyone went mad with excitement as the fish tried to break back through the line. Black heads and shoulders bobbed about and arms thrashed the water as everyone tried to drive the fish away from the gaps and into the nets. At last, with shouting and laughing, the big fishing was over. The lucky fish which had broken through the line were speeding invisibly back to their favourite hiding-places, and the unlucky ones were flopping in the canoes.

Baba and Juma's father and the two boys towed their canoes until they grounded; then they started to count the fish they had caught.

'Your canoe is faster, Rajab,' said Baba to Juma's father; 'it has no outriggers. Let us put all our fish into it, and we will go back together in it. Remember there is the big dance to-night. The children can take back my canoe.'

' Good then,' said Rajab. ' But look out when you are crossing the stream, don't get carried out to sea.'

' That's it,' said Baba. ' Keep near the beach.'

'We know,' said Ali and Juma both together. ' Let us hurry, or we will miss the race back home.'

The fish were soon thrown from Baba's canoe into Rajab's. Ali and Juma set up the two poling-sticks and tied them to the cross-pole of the outrigger nearest the bow. They then fastened the piece of cloth that Baba always took with him to the two sticks and made a sail. All around them other men and boys were doing the same. The last of the day's breeze was still blowing, but it was dying away and there was no time to be lost. The fleet of canoes was soon gliding back with everyone shouting and spurring each other on. In the excitement Ali and Juma had already forgotten their fathers' warning.

' We can never go fast enough near to the shore like this,' said Ali. ' The headland is keeping off the wind, besides, it is shorter to cut across the curve of the beach.'

Gradually they were catching up on the canoes in front, then a steady gust of wind gave them a push which sent them off to the right and close to the reef. The evening breeze started to die away, but they still glided on, looking back in triumph at the others.

Suddenly, shouts came from near the beach. Baba and Rajab were standing up and waving, soon those in the other canoes took up the cry.

' A-ha! They are angry with us for being so far ahead,' chuckled Ali.

'But why are they pointing?' said Juma, puzzled. Then he glanced ahead and gave a frightened cry. He sprang to the sticks which were holding up the sail and started to untie them. 'Quickly!' he cried. 'Undo the sail. Look at the stream!'

Ali scrambled forward to help and caught his breath as he saw the brown, muddy line of the river water a short distance ahead. The river was now rushing down from the distant hills in flood, pouring into the lagoon and making straight out to sea through the gap in the reef.

The canoe was still gliding over the clear lagoon water, but the wind had died away. The boys' only chance was to untie the two sticks and stop the canoe before it reached the rushing stream. Ali tore down the sail and threw it into the bottom of the canoe, then, with Juma, he fumbled with the knots which held the sticks to the cross-pieces. The knots were wet and tight. Juma saw that they would not be able to untie them in time. The canoe had nearly reached the brown water. Perhaps he could reach the bottom with his legs? He threw himself over the side and held on to one of the cross-sticks of the outriggers. His feet reached down, searching for the bottom, but

26

touched nothing. He pulled himself up into the canoe again just as it reached the rushing brown stream. The canoe spun round in the current and drifted with it towards the gap in the reef. The sticks were by now untied, and the boys thrust them down in a feverish attempt to check the canoe. The water was too deep, however, and, in another few moments, their paddleless, rudderless craft was rising to the first wave of the open sea.

Looking back into the lagoon, Ali and Juma could see people who had landed on the reef hurrying along to the gap. They saw their fathers poling Rajab's canoe madly across the stream near the beach. A man on the reef shouted against the noise of the surf, 'Wait for the wind and then sail in again. Do not be afraid.' Then the strong coastwise current swept them out of earshot and they began to drift along, getting ever farther from the reef. Their fathers soon appeared on the reef on the other side of the gap, and the boys could see they were shouting as they waved. They could only wave back with fear in their hearts. The sun was already down behind a line of hills far inland, and was painting the clouds red and pink. The black dots which were their fathers slowly disappeared.

'What shall we do now?' said Juma in a small and miserable voice.

'Wait, that's all,' answered Ali. 'When the wind begins to blow again we will do what that man said. The wind always blows towards the land. When it starts we will put up the sail again, and it will take us back to the shore.'

'But the reef,' said Juma. 'The waves will pick us up and dash us down on it.'

'It is the affair of God,' answered Ali. 'We will try it, that's all.'

'What shall we eat?' said Juma presently.

'What is the use of asking a question like that?' said Ali. 'You know there is nothing—wait though!' he exclaimed, and felt in his pockets.

His hand came on a soft piece of paper, very sticky. He slipped off his shorts and carefully turned the pockets inside out and freed from the lining a very sodden packet of chocolate. It was the packet that the two white boys had given him at the hotel, or what was left of it. Juma fished out his packet.

Carefully the two licked the brown mess off the paper and off their fingers. After gazing for a long time at the now distant shore they wedged themselves down into the bottom of the canoe and covered themselves with the cloth which had served as a sail.

The waves were now as black as ink in the darkness, and seemed oily and warm. The canoe rose and fell—rose and fell. Soon Ali and Juma, in spite of their discomfort, dropped off into an uneasy sleep.

IV

The Ship

ALI was aware, even in his damp, uncomfortable dreams, of the motion of the canoe—up down—up down. Gradually, he was awakened by a bumping under the bows, against which he was leaning, then against the outrigger. He sat up and peered over the side. There was something floating there, like a coco-nut, caught in the cross-pieces. Ali's movement awoke Juma.

' What is it? ' he said.

' I don't know,' said Ali. ' Help me to catch it, it may be something to eat.'

Together, they got the rounded lump into the canoe. It was like a rounded stone, although it floated, and was smooth and hard. The boys tried to taste it, but could not get their teeth into it.

' Let's throw it away,' said Juma.

' No,' said Ali. ' Perhaps it is something useful.'
He dropped it on to the bottom of the canoe.

' Where have we got to? ' asked Juma.

' Here, that's all,' said Ali.

Just then a gleam caught the corner of his eye, but
when he turned round it was gone. Then he caught
it again, a faint light which grew rapidly in size until
it flashed a bright silvery path along the waves right
to the canoe. Then it was gone. After a few seconds
it flashed again.

' It is the light at " In-the-deep-waters " to guide the
big ships,' said Juma. ' The sea has indeed carried us
a long way along the coast.'

' We can see no land,' said Ali. ' So we cannot tell
whether we are opposite " In-the-deep-waters " or not.'

' There is now a little breeze,' said Juma. ' But
where it is blowing to I do not know.'

' It is the breeze before morning,' said Ali.

He looked up at the myriads of stars glowing in the
black velvet sky and then to where he thought the sun
would rise, but could not tell how long it would be to
dawn. For a long time the boys watched the light
flashing, then they dozed off again.

Ali was once more awake, shivering with cold.
A wave had splashed in on his face. Grumbling, he
pulled the cloth over his face and tried to struggle back
to sleep. A sound came to his ears. It was like
people singing a long way off. Was it just a singing
in his head? He opened his eyes and saw there was
a little light filtering through the cloth round his head.

Once more he sat up and peered out—yes—it was getting lighter. It was as light as this yesterday morning when Joogoo, the cock, had woken him up and Baba had sent him out of the house. The wind had started to blow, and must be blowing towards the land. Ali sat up and looked around.

There was the lighthouse, still flashing, but now palely, in the dawn light. On either side of the light he could just make out a dark line which must be the land—but how far away! In the other direction the sky was light green, and a few clouds were touched with pink. Farther round there was a black mass of cloud with thin wisps of rain reaching down like veils to the sea. In the centre the black mass of cloud seemed solid right down to the water and—what was that in front of it, with the faint singing he had heard in his sleep coming from it?

'Wake up you, Juma,' Ali cried, giving Juma a shake. 'There is a ship.'

Ali jumped up, and the two boys gazed towards the black rain cloud. This side of the cloud the dark-grey sea was white with wave-tops and, among their flecks, was a bigger whiteness, like the wing of a huge bird. From this wing came a sound of shouting and singing, very faint, yet real.

'See,' said Ali. 'It is an Arab ship. It is driving towards us in the wind of that rain cloud.'

'I don't like the look of those waves,' said Juma. 'If they strike us like this, with the canoe lying sideways, we will be swamped.'

' We'll put up the sail now,' said Ali. ' Then we'll travel with the waves. The wind will blow us in to land even if the sailors don't see us.'

Hurriedly the two boys tied the sticks once more to the cross-pieces and the cloth to the sticks. As they finished doing this the sea to windward turned dark and the dark patch came rushing towards them. A strong puff of wind struck the sail and bent the sticks forward like reeds. In no time little white waves had sprung up all around, and the canoe, which all night had been floundering like a dead thing, sprang to life and surged along. Then the rain lashed slantingly down and everything was hidden.

Juma knelt down, seized the old tin and began to bale out the water which was now up to his ankles. Ali held tight to the sticks and pulled them back against the wind. At every slight lull he looked round to try to see the sail of the ship and strained his ears to hear any sound, but could see and hear nothing. The waves were by now quite big. Suddenly Juma cried 'Help!' Ali realized that the canoe was now half-full of water. He left go of the sticks and shovelled the water out frantically with his hands. He did not know how long he had been doing this, but, all at once, he found that the lashing rain was now just a drizzle and the wind had dropped to a steady breeze. In front of them now, the black cloud was racing on towards the land, full of wind and white waves. Behind them the sky was clear and blue. The sun was just peeping above the horizon, and there, behind them and to their left, was a sound of singing and a wonderful sight.

A huge sail, like a solid cloud, was billowing out above the brown hull of a big dhow. The mast of the dhow was leaning forward as if the sail could not wait for it to follow. Under the forward-leaning bows there was a mound of white foam which the bows were pushing in front of them over the dark-blue water. The bows rose higher and higher on a wave, then crashed down to send clouds of spray flying up and outwards.

Along the sides of the dhow was a deep fence of matting and, from behind this, came the happy sound of the crew singing some wild song which sounded as if the ship herself was shouting for the joy of sailing and bounding over the sea. Ali and Juma felt that their canoe was rushing along, but this ship was flying, and would very soon overtake and pass them. They shouted and waved, but the huge sail and the fence of matting hid the people in the dhow from view.

The dhow went rushing past until the boys could see the curved inside of the back of the huge sail. Then they saw where the matting ended and the high stern stood up above it. A man dressed in white was sitting up there, holding for all he was worth to the long tiller. The man suddenly turned his head towards the canoe, and his arm went up to answer the waving arms of the boys. The man screamed out something and the singing stopped. A row of black heads, topped with white caps, bobbed up, lining the

matting fence, and arms waved at Ali and Juma.
Still the dhow went thundering on. Wasn't she going
to stop?

As Ali and Juma watched, with growing anxiety,
the headlong rush of the dhow, they saw a tall, thin
man with a green cloth wound round his head appear
by the helmsman. He seemed to glance at the canoe,
then at the sail. Then his arms shot out and shrill
commands came over the water. The black blobs of
faces disappeared from the matting as if by magic,
and their owners could be seen springing to various
ropes about the ship. The big helmsman hauled
with bent body on the tiller. The dhow heeled over
slightly and started to curve round. The billowing
sail started to shiver, and then its beautiful fullness
collapsed and it beat frantically about. Round, and
still farther round came the ship, until her bows were
pointing straight at the canoe. Screams came from
the ship, and then a song shouted out in chorus as the
crew hauled down the sail.

' Quick, Juma,' shouted Ali. ' Take down our sail
too! At this speed we'll shoot past, we can't stop.'

The boys tore down the cloth, and Ali quickly
seized the mooring-rope and stood ready to throw it.
As soon as the cloth was down the canoe became dead
in the water again and started to lurch over the waves,
drifting sideways towards the dhow. The wind still
blew the canoe along, however, and, as luck would
have it, it drifted closer and closer to the ship. As
they were bobbing past Ali threw the rope, which was

at once seized by someone in the dhow, and Ali and
Juma were looking up at a row of laughing faces.

'An affair of what kind of a sort are you?' someone
shouted down to the boys.

'An affair of much hunger, that's all,' Ali shouted
back.

'An affair of too much water,' shouted Juma.

'An affair of too much talk and delay,' screamed a
voice from the high poop. 'Leave off idle words and

35

bring those miserable children of Satan here. You—
Helandogo (Small change), Bicycle, Soap, Bullet—
haul their canoe on board. Ishmael, get the sail up
with the rest of the men. Come on, you children,
jump aboard, don't stand there. Hurry—hurry!'

The high rasping voice was not to be ignored. Ali
and Juma scrambled on board like monkeys. They
stood on the deck looking up at the man with the
green cloth on his head.

The man was tall and thin and wiry. Below the
green head-cloth was a thin yellow face with bushy
black eyebrows and piercing black eyes set rather
close together. A hooked nose, like a hawk's beak,
curved down to a thin cruel mouth. Above the
mouth a black moustache and below a beard which
waggled furiously every time the lean jaws opened to
speak. His spare but wiry frame was covered from
neck to ankles in a white garment. Round his waist
was a broad belt, on the buckle of which was fastened
a beautiful dagger with a silver hilt and a broad L-
shaped scabbard of red leather. This was Haji
Mahmoud bin Musa, the master of the dhow.

The piercing black eyes of Haji gazed down at the
two boys, and seemed to be boring into their brains
until they felt shy and looked down at their shuffling,
wriggling toes.

A shrill scream from Haji made them look up again.
' You are waiting for what—you miserable *goi-
gois ?* ' he shouted. ' Haul up that sail! ' He pointed
a long, skinny hand over the sea. ' Here comes

36

Salim now,' he went on. 'Do you want to lose the cargo at Lamu? You heard what I said at "Haven-of-Peace" and at "Sail". If Salim gets to Lamu first—no pay for anyone. I won't have any money, and you won't get any pay. Haul up that sail!'

Ali and Juma glanced forward towards the mast, where two lines of men were standing, each line with a stout rope running through the hands of the men. The men were facing the mast, at the bottom of which was an enormous pulley-block. From the leading man of each line each rope led through the block and then up the mast and down again to the huge curving yard, from which the sail now hung and lay in folds on the deck.

At the foot of the mast Ishmael, the mate, was screaming at the top of his voice at the two lines of men. His eyes were starting out of his head, and the veins of his neck stood out in his efforts to get the sailors to haul still harder on the ropes.

' Hi-eni—Hi-eni,' Ismael bellowed.

' Hi-eni—Hi-eni,' echoed the tugging men.

' Hi-eni—Hi-eni,' bellowed Ishmael again.

' Hi-eni—Hi-eni,' answered the chorus.

' Haul awa-a-a-a-y,' screamed Ishmael.

' Haul awa-a-a-a-y,' yelled the straining men, as they jerked their bodies in perfect time together on the ropes, and the yard and sail creaked a few feet higher up the mast.

As they finished the heave Ishmael shouted, ' Hold fast ! ' Then he started again. ' Hi-eni—Hi-eni . . . '

Ali and Juma glanced out over the sea to where Haji had pointed when he said that Salim was coming up. There was another huge white sail pounding another brown hull through the dark-blue water, heading straight towards them with spray flying each time the sharp bows hacked down into a wave.

By the time the boys had gazed their full at Salim's plunging ship a yell came from Ishmael: ' Sail ready.' Haji turned quickly to the steersman and said in a quiet voice—quite different from his screaming commands to the crew—' Get going, never mind where Salim sails. Get to windward of him. The ship can do it.'

' That's it,' said the helmsman, a huge black man with a round and contented face, as he pushed over the tiller. There was a crack like thunder overhead as the sail filled suddenly with wind. The ship heeled over until it seemed as if the sea would pour in through the matting along the leeward gunwale.

But the water started to flow past, the ship righted herself, and soon she was surging forward once more; not fast enough, however, to hold off the rival dhow.

The rush of Salim's bow wave could be heard as he swooped down on Haji, passing a few yards to windward. As Salim's sail surged alongside, the sail of Haji's dhow gave a loud flap as Salim's sail stole its wind. Then it filled again with a boom, but the flap had given a momentary check to Haji's ship.

A hail came from Salim, a white-robed stately figure.

'You are doing what, Haji, fishing?' he called mockingly.

Haji's eyes flashed with anger, but he answered with a high laugh, 'Yes, I've caught two young fish here. I've time to catch fish—and the cargo in Lamu too. What have you been doing all night, Salim, sleeping?' Haji's crew yelled with delight at their skipper's wit.

Then came Salim's voice. 'Yes, we slept soundly all night and recovered our strength, hence our present speed. Farewell Haji! I don't suppose we shall meet again for some time. I'll send my men out from Lamu to tow you in.'

This time it was from Salim's ship that a roar of laughter came, followed by quick hand-clapping in an intricate rhythm. A rousing chorus was fitted into the time of the hand claps.

> 'Ho—yohoho!' (Clap-a-clap-a-clap.)
> 'Ho—yohoho!' (Clap-a-clap-a-clap.)

Then a high quavering voice began to make up a song about the speed of Salim's ship, which was like a bird, and Haji's ship, which was like a log. After each line of the rude song came:

' Ho—yohoho ! ' (Clap-a-clap-a-clap.)

fainter and fainter as Salim's ship slid ahead.

' Sons of dogs,' spat out Haji. Then he laughed and said to the helmsman up on the poop: ' Get the sail full of wind and then keep to windward. Salim's never heard of windward. This breeze won't last all day, and then we'll have to catch the wind from rain clouds, as we did when these two bad boys spoiled the race.' He bent his piercing black eyes on Ali and Juma again. ' Come here, you—I want to talk to you.'

V

The Mysterious Lump

ALI and Juma went closer to Haji and stood before him. Haji's long, skinny fingers clawed out and clutched each boy by the shoulder. He was about to speak to them, when shouts and a clattering noise came from just forrard of where they were standing. Helandogo, Bicycle, Soap, and Bullet had just hauled Baba's canoe on board and dumped it down on the deck with much shouting and fuss.

Haji strode to the canoe, and the two boys followed to see if it was still intact.

'Too much noise!' snapped Haji to the four men. 'Get forrard.'

Haji glanced into the canoe and saw only the two punting-sticks, an old fruit tin, a very wet piece of cloth, and a round, brownish lump lying in the

bottom. He sniffed contemptuously, and was about
to sit on the edge of the canoe facing Ali and Juma
when he turned and looked down again at the lump.
He reached down into the canoe and picked the lump
up and stood for some time with his back to the two
boys, but they could tell by the movements of his
elbows that Haji was turning the lump over and over
in his hands, and by his bent forward head that he
was looking intently at it. At last he turned to Ali
and Juma and said, with a jerk of his beard to the
short ladder which led to the poop:

'Follow me up there.'

Haji sat on the bulwark of the poop, and the quick
eyes of the boys noticed that his long, thin fingers
were still clutching the lump. Then the boys looked
at Haji's face and saw something in it that had not
been there before. Ali saw at once the eyes of
Squidface the bully, his enemy in the village, when he
was thinking of something unpleasant to do to him.
Juma remembered the eyes of a snake he had once
seen, bright and glittering, gazing at a frog, frozen
with fear a few inches away, just before the snake
lashed forward its poisonous fangs.

Haji's face twisted itself into what was meant for a
smile.

'Where do you boys live?' he asked.

'Near the village of the francolin,' said Ali.

'And where is that?' asked Haji patiently.

'It is on the coast, between "In-the-deep-waters"
and "Place-of-the-cave,"' said Ali.

' Are you brothers? '

' No. We are friends, not brothers.'

' How did you come to be in the middle of the sea in this canoe? '

' We were swept away by a swift river, and have been in the sea all night.'

' You have fathers? '

' Yes, our fathers were in another canoe.'

' They saw you swept away? '

' They saw us swept away but could not help us.'

Then Juma said, ' We wish to return quickly to our fathers and mothers.'

Haji looked sharply at Juma.

' That you cannot do! By stopping to pick you up I have already lost time. I must reach Lamu before Salim.' Haji glanced over the sea to the gleam that was Salim's sail. ' I stopped to pick you up, saved you from death, am I to lose the cargo at Lamu to Salim? No, you must come with me to Lamu, there you will go ashore, and then you can go home.'

Ali answered quickly, ' Lamu is far—far! How can we reach home from there? ' Then he said, ' My Baba's canoe—we will take it back—how? '

' Your own affair,' said Haji. ' Am I your father and mother that I must look after you for the rest of your lives? What else do you want—eh? '

' We want food,' said Juma, and Ali realized that his insides were aching with hunger.

43

'Allah!' exclaimed Haji. 'In a moment of madness I stop to save your worthless lives and let Salim get ahead in the race to Lamu, and now you ask for food! You must work for food. Ishmael will give you work. Badfish will give you food. Go to the galley and get food.'

Something made Ali think that they would not be on the poop again. He glanced down at the lump of stuff still held in Haji's lap, then up into Haji's eyes.

'Well?' said Haji.

'That thing,' faltered Ali. 'It is a thing of what sort?'

'This?' said Haji, looking at the lump as if for the first time. 'Oh—this—it is nothing—stuff that floats in the sea. Some say it is the dung of some sea-animal.' He laughed carelessly and tossed the lump into a coil of rope, rubbed his hands, then turned fiercely on Ali. With his thin fingers he pushed both boys towards the steps. 'Get forrard, you two, and don't come up here again,' he grated out through his thin lips, then, 'Watch your steering, son of a dog,' to the huge black helmsman, whose wide-apart, contented eyes had strayed for a moment to the coil of rope in which the worthless lump now rested.

Ali and Juma went from the bottom of the steps to the canoe and took out of it their cloth. As Ali bent down to pick up the cloth he noticed that a small piece of the lump, which must have broken off, was

44

lying in the bottom of the canoe. A quick impulse
make him pick it up and slip it into his pocket.

From above, Haji's harsh voice came. ' Ishmael,
give these miserable brats food, then give them work,
and get this firewood '—he pointed to the canoe—
' up there with the long-boat.'

VI

The Little Old Ship's Cook

ALI and Juma stumbled forrard over the legs and
bodies of men who were lying about on the deck,
until they came to a little square shack, with a big
iron water-tank beside it, which was the galley.
Inside the galley, at the back, a little old man, with
silvery threads in the woolly twists of his hair, was
squatting over a charcoal brazier.

As the two boys looked down at him, feeling very
weak and empty, a smell of frying fish came to their
nostrils, and they realized that they were nearly
fainting with hunger. Their shadows fell across the
doorway, and the old man looked up and they saw
a wrinkled face with the cheekbones standing out
below two bright eyes. The eyes screwed up and the
loose mouth opened in a friendly grin of a few odd
teeth and pink gums.

'Come on, children,' the little old man cackled.

'Come in here—or perhaps you don't want any food—eh?'

Ali and Juma almost fell into the galley in their hurry and shyly squatted down opposite the old man. The bright, bird-like eyes looked from one pinched young face to the other, and the little lines at the corners crinkled up in a smile.

'I see that you perceive much hunger—that's not good—but soon you'll be complete again.'

The little old man reached a skinny arm out to a big pot and to two bowls. He dipped the bowls into the pot, and then handed one each to Ali and Juma.

'Porridge with much sugar first,' the little old man cackled. 'By this road you will receive strength to defeat these fish.' He pointed to the brazier. 'I am called Badfish, and that is in truth the name I was given as a babe, but these fish which *chachatika* here in the oil did not die when I was named but only this morning.

'You have finished already?' gabbled the little old cook. 'Give me the bowls.' He dipped them in the big pot again and handed them back. 'Now then, this time—slowly—slowly, gently—hurry-hurry has no blessing. A-ha!—that's the way. Your strength has been returned to you—not so?'

The thin, warm gruel, nearly all sugar, was acting like magic on Ali and Juma, and their skins were already less grey. The smell of the frying fish no longer brought an almost unbearable ache to their tummies, but was just the most delicious thing in the

47

world, together with their furious merry *chachatika*
noise as they frizzled. They now had strength to
speak, and even to grin slightly as they murmured:

' It is very good. Since yesterday morning up to
now we have not eaten.'

The little old cook chattered on as the boys fell to
on the fish, and soon Ali and Juma felt strong and
happy and were telling Badfish how they were swept
out to sea, and describing their night of cold and
misery and their rescue. As they talked, Helandogo,
Bicycle, Soap and Bullet, who had by now stowed
Baba's canoe beside the dhow's long-boat, were standing round the door listening. Every now and then
one of the sailors would exclaim ' A-la!' or give a
sharp ' Eh!' of astonishment. Ali and Juma knew
now that they were indeed heroes.

' It is the affair of God. God is indeed good,' said
little old Badfish cheerfully at last, and the rest all
cried:

' That's it—God truly fixed up this affair, if he had
not you would have been drowned.'

' But your Babas and Mamas will be thinking
what?' suddenly asked Badfish, and Ali and Juma
no longer felt like heroes.

There were groans and shakings of heads from the
sailors. Although the two boys could not imagine
that their parents would think that they were dead,
since they themselves knew that they were alive, they
felt solemn and uncomfortable.

Ali glanced outside at Baba's canoe and said,

48

'We will return like how? I don't know. My Baba will see much bitterness because his canoe is lost.' Ali fell silent at the thought of all their difficulties. At last he hung his head and muttered miserably, 'I cannot arrive in front of my Baba without the canoe. He will say what? I don't know.'

'Eh! It is a difficult business, truly-truly,' said Helandogo, and everyone shook his head and clicked his tongue and pondered deeply.

At last Badfish cleared his throat and said in an important voice, 'There is but one road that I can see.' He paused impressively to make sure that all eyes were upon him. 'One road, that's all, finish! I know it because I am old.'

'A road of what kind of a sort, old one? Say it,' said Bullet impatiently.

'Wait, you,' said Badfish. 'And listen all of you, and in a little you will perceive my intelligence.'

Someone sighed heavily and groaned. Everyone started laughing at Badfish's self-importance.

Bullet stopped laughing first and shouted, 'Silence all. Listen to the old one. How can he speak when you laugh?' Then Bicycle stopped laughing and shouted for silence, and then Helandogo and Soap told Bicycle and Bullet to shut up. At last all ears were bent towards Badfish.

The little old cook kept silent with an offended look on his face for as long as he dared. Then he went on.

'When we arrive at Lamu,' said Badfish, 'it will be necessary for these two children to go to the Mister

49

District Commissioner or to the Mister Police and make reporti.'

No one else had thought of this easy solution, and each was angry with himself for being so stupid, and annoyed with Badfish for thinking of it first.

'Of course, everyone knows that that is necessary,' they cried, and Helandogo, who thought that Badfish was just a silly old man, said:

'And then what? If you go to the police they begin to think out what sort of crime you must have done. If a man has done no crime he is of no interest to the police, therefore it is necessary for them to name a crime for him.'

'Yes,' said Bullet. 'And while they are thinking about you they lock you up in the maboose so that they are not disturbed by the thought of you running away.'

'Sometimes they perceive much difficulty in discovering your wickedness, and you stay in the maboose for many months,' said Soap.

'That's it,' said Bicycle. 'Then you are brought in front of the Mister D.C., and he says the Government is unable to prove your wickedness and you have permission to return to your home—but by that time,' he added, 'you are too old to obtain work.'

A roar of laughter greeted this last remark, but Badfish screamed angrily, 'All right then, if you are all afraid to go to the police. Go to the Mister D.C.'

'It is not we who are going to see a European but these boys,' said Helandogo.

'That's it,' said Bullet. 'And how will they be able to appear in front of the Mister D.C.?'

'It is indeed difficult,' said Bicycle. 'If they hang about outside the Mister D.C.'s office they will be driven away by the clerks.'

'That's true,' said Soap. 'Even grown men are despised by clerks.'

'Clerks are indeed men of great importance, and by their intelligence they can defeat people who wish to bring their affairs to the Mister D.C.'

'And again,' said Bullet, 'if clerks despise grown men, how much more will a Mister D.C. despise two small boys—they are nothing in his eyes.'

'You are all saying the words of fools,' screamed out old Badfish. 'Also you are saying bad words about the Government. Are you unable to perceive shame?'

This aroused a storm of anger from the rest.

'Who is capable of saying bad things about the Government?' they cried, to which Badfish answered hotly:

'I suppose no one said anything about the police just now, are they not the men of the Government?'

'Oh, that,' the rest replied. 'We were just talking, that's all, about the customs of the police. To say that we were saying anything bad is a lie. The Government is the affair of Kingi George, do people exist who say bad things about him?'

'Very well then,' said Badfish, apparently satisfied with this queer explanation and eager to hold forth again. 'There are people here who say these boys will not be able to arrive in front of the Mister D.C. because of the clerks. Truly-truly,' he went on, 'it is an affair which can only be fixed up by one of intelligence who has much experience of the hearts of Europeans of importance.'

'Such as you, I suppose?' asked Helandogo, and the rest jeered and laughed.

'Keep quiet—all of you!' yelled Badfish, and then went on in a reasonable and condescending tone, 'Keep quiet please and I will tell you. Perhaps you think I have spent all my years cooking in this dhow, but no! I was once the kitchen-child in the house of the Mister D.C. in Strife, and I know the road to the heart of a European. For these children it is easier than for a grown man.'

Badfish saw that he now had the attention of his listeners, and went on with great importance.

'What these children must do when they reach Lamu, is to go to the Mister D.C.'s own house and watch until the Mister returns from his office. Then, they must watch until the kitchen-child has gone on some errand and cannot drive them away for fear they obtain his work. Then these children must go to the cook and speak to him as children of good manners asking for work.

'After the cook has said that there is no work for them they must say that theirs is not an affair of hunting work but an affair of much trouble. If God helps them the cook will listen to their story. He will

52

be astonished and call the house-boy to hear it also. Then these children will ask if it is possible for their affair to be taken to the Mister D.C., as there is no one to help them.

'The cook and house-boy will talk together, and the house-boy will enter the house to measure the heart of his master to see whether it is fierce or easy. At first, the Mister will be hot and tired. Then he will have a bath and put on comfortable clothes and come out and sit on the veranda.

'The house-boy will make a noise inside the house with bottles of strong drink and glasses and bring them out to the Mister before he grows impatient, and the Mister will be pleased. While the Mister is drinking, the house-boy will not go away, as is his custom, but will hang about until the Mister puts down his glass and sighs. Then the house-boy will shuffle about with his feet, and the Mister will say sharply, "You want what?"

'The house-boy will be used to the sharp words of his master, and will not be afraid, but will say, "There is one small affair, Bwana." The Mister D.C. will groan heavily, like one driven near to madness, and say, "An affair of what sort?" The house-boy will say, "Not an affair of work, Bwana. An affair of two children who are in great trouble and have only escaped because God has helped them. Now they pray that you also will follow the example of God and help them, as their parents think they are dead." House-boys are rogues completely, but they are experts in measuring the hearts of their Bwanas.

' After these words of the house-boy the Bwana will speak to these children, but at the end he will say, " I can help you like how? I can't help you. The Government can't give money to all the children who *tanga-tanga* about the country." Then these children will see great bitterness because the Bwana D.C. will not help them. But, as they are leaving, the Bwana will say in a very fierce voice, " Arrive in front of me in my office to-morrow." Then he will call the house-boy and in a fierce voice he will tell him to give the children food and a place to sleep.

' The children may then rejoice exceedingly. They need have no fear that the Bwana will not help them to return to their homes.'

Badfish looked round triumphantly, and his audience laughed at his summing-up of the character of a Bwana D.C. Then they turned to the two boys—but Ali and Juma were fast asleep.

VII

The Long Race by Day

THE dhow sped rapidly on all through the long day. The fresh wind was blowing so steadily that there was little for the crew to do. The huge sail was set to the best advantage to get the utmost from the wind, and the helmsman was the only one on board who could help the ship on her course.

Far off, on the landward side and forward of Haji's ship, Salim's sail was a white speck on the horizon. Salim was making straight for Lamu in the race for the cargo, trusting to the wind to blow him right into the port. Haji was keeping farther out to sea, gambling on the wind giving out before Salim could reach Lamu. In the morning, when the wind started to blow again, it would reach his sail first and give his ship a flying start. Any rain-cloud which came on him in the night would give him the same advantage. There was nothing to do now, therefore, but leave the present wind, the beautiful lines of the dhow and the skill of the helmsman to work together to drive the ship along.

Most of the crew were lying about here and there, wrapped in light-brown blankets, as still and lifeless as bundles of old clothes. Badfish was trailing a line over the side and occasionally pulling in a leaping, struggling fish. Ali and Juma were still fast asleep in the hot, sheltered cooking-place. Haji and Ishmael the mate seemed to have forgotten all about them, although Haji most certainly had not.

In the afternoon, when the swaying shadow of the sail was beginning to creep more and more into the ship, things suddenly began to happen. A cry from the helmsman brought Haji on to the poop from his cramped shelter underneath it. In no time Ishmael's eyes were starting out of his head as he yelled at the lifeless bundles of blankets to arise. The noise and bustle and the arrival of Badfish in his galley awoke even Ali and Juma, who scrambled up, fresh and alert.

Little old Badfish chuckled as he got a sheet of metal from the floor and placed it over his brazier.

' Haji's luck ! ' he cackled. ' Hee—hee—heeeeeee ! Much wind is coming to help him, with rain also— see over there ! '

He pointed out to starboard. The boys jumped up and ran to the matting at the side of the ship and peered over the top.

The whole of the horizon to windward was hidden in a blue, dark-grey curtain, and the inky-blue sea in front of it was turning to blue-black. The sun was still blazing down on the ship. Suddenly, the bellying sail flapped and filled again. The noise of the ship through the waves took on a quieter note, as if she was listening for something. Then the air grew colder and damper and a glorious rainbow towered up into the sky. Ali and Juma could almost see the exact wave, not very far from them, from which the rainbow sprang. As they watched the place a huge dark shape broke the surface and sent up a fountain of fine spray, then sank again into the sea.

' Nyangumi—the whale! ' several sailors shouted, and all looked eagerly over the sea to be the first to see him again.

The bellowing of Ishmael cut short this whale-spotting, and soon everyone was standing by the ropes in readiness. Haji, after a long, searching glance at the exact position of Salim's white speck of a sail in the distance, stood quietly facing the approaching wind.

Ishmael shouted, ' Every man stand in his place. Follow my orders exactly. Let no man follow his own intelligence, let him follow my orders. In this way only can we hope to catch up with Salim. Let no man make a mistake, or his share in the voyage will be cut for spoiling the share of the others.'

' That's it! ' cried the sailors.

They were as anxious as anyone else to beat Salim into Lamu, as the amount of money each man would receive at Aden would depend on how much cargo they could take there. They also wished to avenge the insults shouted at them and the rude song sung at them by Salim's crew as they passed their ship in the morning.

Haji still stood high up in the stern, watching calmly but intently the rapidly approaching storm. Soon a dark patch came rushing towards the dhow over the surface of the water. As it reached her a cold gust of wind, with fine rain in it, struck the skin of every man on board. The sail filled out with a bang. The ship began to surge forward, and Haji made a quick move with his hand to the steersman and a quiet order. He had judged the quarter from which the storm would strike. The helmsman moved the long tiller, and the ship began to swing round in the direction of Salim's distant sail. A quick scream to Ishmael from Haji, and the mate sprang into action with shouts to the crew to pay out the main-sheet.

In the next instant the full force of the storm struck the dhow like a blow and heeled her over. The sail looked as if it would burst with the pressure of wind or tear the curving tapering yard from the creaking mast. It was as if cruel spurs had been jabbed into a fiery horse. The dhow plunged forward and, in a few seconds, seemed to be tearing through the water. Haji peered under the sail to get a last glimpse of Salim's position and point out his course to the helmsman before everything was blotted out by the coming rain.

Even Ali and Juma, who had never been to sea before, could understand what was happening. From the moment Salim had passed him in the morning, Haji had been waiting for this chance to make up what he had lost by stopping to pick up the boys. All day he had been working his ship to windward of Salim, while keeping him in sight. If this storm had not come he would have been almost certain to have lost the race to Lamu. But it had come, and now he hoped to rush down with the wind on Salim and catch him up—or even pass him. At any rate he could close in on Salim before night-fall, and so things would at least be equal between them till morning came. The force of the wind was terrific—but would it last for long enough? Or was it just one of those sudden squalls which rush towards Africa and then are gone as quickly as they have come? Haji might know, but Ali and Juma could not.

The two boys were filled with excitement. They felt, for the first time, that they were a part of the charging ship, the crew, the big helmsman, and so— strangely—of Haji! Everyone in the dhow had only one thought—the ship and the race she was running— and so everyone, from the cruel master to the two small passengers, were for the moment, one.

The rain still held off, and the dhow still rushed over the waves. Ishmael kept glancing up at the yard and the thick circle of rope which held it to the mast. He went to the stout rope shrouds which came down from the mast-head to either side of the ship and which helped to take the strain of the tugging of the sail that could snap even the stout tree from which the mast was made.

Ishmael held the shrouds and tried to bend them

towards him, but they remained as straight as bars of
iron. He seemed satisfied, but glanced often aloft at
the parrel, which kept the yard in its place against
the top of the mast. If anything parted now the race
was lost, and he would be blamed for not having seen
to it that it was strong enough to bear any strain.

The crew gazed out intently over the bows to try to
pick out Salim, but the fine rain which had passed
over formed a curtain between the two dhows. The
helmsman had to steer blind and trust to his instinct.

On and on rushed the dhow, her sharp bows pressed
down by the sail into the water, which ploughed up in
white foam under her forefoot and slid away aft to
leave a long, straight line as far as the eye could follow
it. Suddenly, Helandogo, up in the bows, gave a yell
' There ! ' and pointed slightly to his left. At once,
all were shouting and pointing. Through the haze
a white triangle could be seen, quite close. There,
just where Haji had planned, was Salim's sail! At
least Haji was level with his rival now, even slightly
ahead. From now on the better ship, the better crew,
and the better captain would win the race to Lamu.

By this time the wind had reached Salim's ship,
which was heeling over on the point of sailing which
is the fastest of all, with the wind blowing across the
ship. Haji's ship had been speeding down with the
wind and, if she went on, would pass just in front of
Salim's bows. The sooner Haji got on to the same
course and held his slight lead (keeping to windward,
where he was now), the better.

His usual quick word to the helmsman and a high,
wind-piercing order to the mate made the dhow
swing round at the same instant that some of the crew
flung themselves on the sheet rope to haul the sail
tighter in to the ship. They hauled with quick, short
jerks on the rope in perfect time. As the wind now
struck the sail sideways, instead of from the stern, as
before, the dhow gave a great lurch, almost on to her
beam ends. Ali and Juma were flung against the
matting sides and thought that the ship would turn
right over. Water was raging just below their feet.
They were looking straight down at the flecks of foam
streaking past. After the first blow, however, the
dhow swung back to a less perilous-seeming angle
and settled down at once to pick up her fastest pace.

Now that they were both on the same course, it could
be seen exactly how the two ships were placed. Haji
was slightly ahead, but Salim was gaining—gaining.
Then Haji's ship got into her full stride on her new
course, and Salim stayed where he was, slightly astern.

Haji's crew, and Ali and Juma with them, cheered
and sang and clapped their hands and hopped up and
down in time to their own music; a dance of joy at the
thrill of this wonderful race. Then, at last, the rain,
which had been pushing the wind along, came down
with stinging force. The two dhows were blotted
out of sight of each other in a moment. Little old
Badfish could be heard screaming with rage as the
raindrops spat and *chachatika-ed* on his brazier and
threatened to put it out.

VIII

It is Ambari !

THE rain was gone as quickly as it had come, and the wind also went with it, leaving a breeze of about the same strength as before the sudden storm. Both dhows were still clipping along, but without the furious drive which had heeled them so far over before the rain came down. They were running more easily under less pressure of wind, and still held the same positions as before.

The high clouds were now tinged with pink by the rapidly setting sun, and the two huge sails caught the pink from the clouds. Soon, the breeze came and went in fitful gusts, then, as the sun sank behind a vast bank of flame-edged cloud, it died to a gentle breath that could scarcely be felt. Soap, on orders from Ishmael, carried a huge lighted lantern forrard from Haji's quarters and hoisted it up on the forestay. A pale gleam shone from Salim's dhow, and the tiny curved sliver of silver of a new moon shone in the sky just above the bank of cloud.

The dhows were now like two ghost ships gliding over the dark sea. Even in this gentle breath of air the sails were still drawing, as the sigh-sigh of parted water under the bows showed.

Haji, Ishmael and those others who were Mahommedans were now engaged in their solemn, silent evening prayers. All faced the bows, which were roughly heading in the direction of Mecca, their holy city, thousands of miles away over sea and land. First, they stood with bent heads, motionless. Then, after they had repeated in their thoughts the first sacred words of praise to Allah, they bowed until their hands touched their knees for the second words of prayer. Again they stood upright and bowed again twice more. Lastly, they sank down on their knees and, with long pauses between each obeisance, bent down until their foreheads touched the mats or blankets which they had spread carefully before them, then rose again to their knees. They were now as near to Allah as each man's love of God could take him. From these most solemn prostrations they rose again, as if slowly withdrawing from the presence of God, step by step, back into their hard seafaring life.

The Christians and Pagans were hushed into quiet by this stately mystery, and it was some time before the whole crew became its noisy, lively self again.

A warm glow came from Badfish's galley. Ali and Juma moved over to it.

'May we come in?' Juma said timidly.

'Come in, children!' called Badfish, 'and help to

64

stir the porridge. Afterwards you can take it round
to the men.'

After the bowls of porridge and then of fish had
been eaten, the crew sat round in little groups, talking
and laughing over the events of the day. Helandogo
produced from somewhere a small piece of board on
to which were fastened small, flat steel springs which
curved up slightly. With deft fingers Helandogo
touched these springs and let them go again and so
made a melodious music. Each spring had its own
soft note, and, as Helandogo settled down to the tune
he was making up, the notes ran into each other as if
water was falling on to tiny silvery drums. On and
on went the soft, scarcely audible, watery music.

From Salim's dhow a long, sad song came rolling
over the sea, followed by a happy chorus accompanied
by hand-clapping to a fascinating rhythm. Then
Bicycle came to the fore with a battered old guitar
and strummed a fierce, exciting, wandering tune.
Bullet and Soap seized two old tins and, holding them
under their left arms, began to beat them madly with
fluttering fingers. The rest of the crew picked up the
song until the night was full of voices and music.
Through it all the yard creaked to the gently swaying
mast, and the bow-wave sighed and was silent, sighed
and was silent.

Ali and Juma were sitting, happily drowsy in the
warmth of Badfish's brazier, when its glow lit up the
serene face of the man whom they had first seen in the
early morning, the huge helmsman, who now greeted

Badfish and squatted down for his meal. He gave
the boys a smile and turned to Badfish to receive his
bowl of food. Ali and Juma noticed that a small
silvery cross glinted on his broad chest.

' Ah-ha, Manowari! ' said Badfish, as he handed
over the bowl. ' You did well to-day at the tiller.
Salim thought what when he saw our ship flying down
on him, like a sea-eagle on a fish? From the time we
saw Nyangumi, the whale, until the wind failed you
did well truly-truly.'

' It was the affair of God, that's all,' said Manowari
in his cheerful resonant voice. ' When I was in the
Navy in the war I was taught to steer straight. If the
ship had not arrived close to Salim's, as Haji ordered,
I would have perceived great shame—and then you
would have said what, old one? '

Badfish laughed and shook his head.

Ali plucked up courage and said, ' There is a small
question.'

Badfish blinked kindly at him. ' A question of what
sort, child? '

' That Nyangumi is a thing of what kind? ' Ali
asked.

' Nyangumi! ' exclaimed Manowari. ' He is not
a small question. He is a very big question completely; nearly the length of this ship and having the
strength of many elephants.'

The two boys pondered on the immense size of
whales for a bit.

Then Juma asked, ' What do they eat, is it sharks? '

'No—not sharks,' said Manowari. 'But many fish, who can tell how many? Nyangumi is indeed a wonder of the sea. I met a man once who had been down to South Africa and worked in a big town on the coast where whales are cut up and their flesh is made into oil.'

'But how are they caught—who can catch a thing of that size?' Ali asked with goggling eyes.

'There are small steamships that the whale-catchers use,' said Manowari, 'and in their bows are guns that fire spears. Nyangumi must come up to breathe, like Kiboko, the hippopotamus. When he comes up to the surface a spear is fired into him. The spear has a long rope fastened to it, and to the ship, and so Nyangumi is caught. However hard he struggles to escape, the rope holds him until his breath gives out. At last he is killed, and his body is pulled to the shore. My friend cut up many whales and saw how the flesh was boiled until the oil ran out, enough to fill many barrels. In this way the white men make much profit.'

'That's it,' said Badfish. 'And there is another great profit to be had from the whale; but this profit does not come from hunting or by work but through the blessing of God on him who finds it.'

'You mean ambari?' said Manowari slowly.

He looked quickly round, as if to see whether anyone was listening. His wide eyes rested at last on the intent faces of the two boys.

'That's it, ambari,' said Badfish. 'It is something

that comes from the stomach of Nyangumi and is at last cast on the shore by the waves. Lucky is he who finds ambari. Though small, its value is very great.'

' It looks like what? ' The question burst from Ali and Juma together, and their bodies were bent forward and faces thrust out in their eagerness.

Badfish looked at the boys and was pleased at the interest they seemed to be taking. Manowari was looking at the two and smiling slightly, but his eyes also held excitement. Then Badfish laughed.

' If I had found ambari would I be a cook in this dhow? No! But God is good,' he added. ' Had I found ambari I would be dead from the knife of some thief or from too much to drink. There is danger, as well as profit, to him who finds ambari. No, I have never seen ambari, but I know it is used for many things.'

' For medicine? ' asked Juma.

' Aye,' said Badfish. ' Mostly by women whose husbands are wealthy. It is said that, if one is thin and wasting away, one must go into the sea when it is returning to the land. As the water rises one must eat some ambari and, in a little while, one's body will become firm and rounded. Those who are burdened with too much fat, must stand in the sea when the tide is full and eat ambari. Then, as the water draws away from the land, so will the fat be drawn away from the body.' Badfish looked down at his skinny self and said, ' When you see me standing in the sea, chewing like a cow, then you will know that I have found ambari and am about to become handsome and strong, like Manowari.'

The boys laughed with delight at this idea, but neither they nor Badfish nor Manowari knew that their laugh had attracted Helandogo, Bullet, Bicycle and Soap to the edge of the brazier's glow. Helandogo's softly tinkling instrument ceased its water-music, and the four men listened, hoping to catch some of Badfish's funny remarks.

Manowari stroked the back of his neck thoughtfully.

' Only people of backwardness believe such things, but many know that it is used by the very rich to burn for incense. It makes a pleasant smell in their houses. I myself have perceived this smell in Zanzibar. I was passing the house of a very rich Arab when a smell caught in my nose. I asked the doorkeeper, " A smell of what sort, Mister? " And he replied, " Ambari—the cost of one sniff is equal to my wages for a month." And I said, " Then I must run to the market and sell my breath before I breathe again," and passed on.'

Ali and Juma were, by now, trembling with excitement. Ali felt in his pocket and pulled out the broken-off piece of the lump he had found in the bottom of the canoe when he picked out the cloth. By now, the piece had broken into crumbs. Among them, on Ali's palm, was a beak-like thing, the beak of a squid. Ali held the pieces out to Manowari.

' Is this ambari? ' he asked.

' I do not know from my own intelligence,' said

Manowari, 'but the look on Haji's face when he saw that lump this morning and said it was as nothing tells me now that it is.'

'We can burn a bit in the brazier and then you can smell it and tell us if it has the smell you smelt in Zanzibar,' Juma said with shining eyes.

Manowari looked round, but did not see the four listeners duck back into the darkness.

'Let us try with a little crumb,' he whispered. 'Even a small piece will fill the ship with its smell.' Manowari took a tiny crumb from Ali's pink palm and put it near a little spark of charcoal which had fallen from the brazier on to the sheet of metal on which the brazier stood. Carefully, he pushed the crumb towards the spark until they touched. A little curl

of smoke arose. Manowari bent right down and sniffed at it, then clapped his hand down on to it to put it out. He coughed, and sat upright again. 'It *is* ambari.'

He raised his eyes to think what this meant—and looked straight into the glinting eyes of Helandogo, Bullet, Bicycle and Soap.

For a long moment there was a heavy silence, then Helandogo's teeth flashed into a wide, open grin.

'We have heard everything,' he said. 'Haji has got the children's ambari—now we will do what?'

'It is not your affair,' said Manowari sharply.

Helandogo laughed. 'Not our affair? To get this ambari from Haji you think you will just go up to him and say, " I want the children's ambari," and he will hand it over?'

Manowari thought for a minute.

'Yes, that is what I will do,' he said. 'And I will not need anyone else to help me to say it. One voice will be enough.'

'And Haji will say what?' asked Helandogo.

'When I ask for the ambari,' replied Manowari, 'Haji will hand it to me. I will ask for it just as the Customs men are coming aboard.'

Helandogo gazed sorrowfully at Manowari and then let out a long, sighing groan.

'Eeeeeh—you are like what? I don't know. Are we all to be handcuffed and shut up while the police think up what we have all done? Salim is to get the cargo while we lose everything through delay?'

Manowari was silent, and Helandogo pressed on, 'No—we must talk much before we reach Lamu.'

Badfish, quiet for so long, shook his grizzled head and spat into the brazier.

'There is danger, as well as profit, in ambari,' he mumbled sadly.

Manowari looked steadily and calmly at Helandogo and his three friends.

'If you wish to talk—come near and talk,' he said.

After the four genial scoundrels had squatted down round the brazier Helandogo began earnestly :

'We are all black people here?' he said. 'The rest in this ship are Arabs. Are we to be defeated by Arabs, or are we to lose our share in the profits of the voyage through the delays of the servants of the Government? No! We must all work together and fix up this affair so that we black people seize the ambari and the voyage is not delayed. Is it not so?'

Bullet, Bicycle and Soap chorused, 'It is so!' with much conviction.

'Well then,' went on Helandogo—but Manowari cut in:

'The ambari belongs to the children, it is their property.'

'And the children can get it back by themselves?' asked Helandogo. 'You, Manowari, and you, Badfish—you seek no profit for helping the children?' He laughed sarcastically. 'You help them for nothing—eh?'

'We have not yet mentioned profit to the children,'

72

said Manowari loftily. 'The children have confided in us. You only stole upon us and listened. Heh children, is it not so?'

Ali and Juma, still recovering from the shock of Helandogo and his friends discovering their secret, could only shake their heads and say miserably, 'I don't know.' 'I am unable to say anything.'

'You see!' said Helandogo triumphantly. 'They are but children. Think well, if there is trouble over the ambari you will need witnesses to say that the ambari was indeed in the children's canoe. We are your witnesses; without us your case will be defeated.'

Manowari at last said heavily, 'I agree, we will make a plan.'

Little old Badfish sat very still and gazed into the glow of his brazier, and all forgot about him.

The talk went on and on between Manowari and Helandogo, with occasional remarks and grunts from the other three. The two boys, worn out with excitement, fell asleep while the dhow rose and fell, creaked and sighed, through the velvety night.

IX

Fighting and Racing

ALI and Juma were woken by Ishmael shouting at the men in the galley. 'Leave off this noise—Helandogo and all of you—get out of here—there is no permission for you to be in the kitchen—Manowari and the children may remain.' The four men grinned cheerfully and disappeared to their rough sleeping-places on the hard deck.

Manowari looked out to make sure they had really gone, then turned to Badfish and said softly, 'You think what, old one?'

Badfish cackled to himself, then frowned and shook his head at himself, then said, 'I don't know.' Then, 'Maybe—I don't know.'

'Speak sense, old one! You are saying what?' Manowari said impatiently.

Badfish took no notice, but went on muttering to himself. At last he seemed to clear his mind of whatever was worrying him and said, 'Follow the road you have agreed upon with those rascals. Now,' he said, 'we have talked of the uses of ambari, we have smelt the smell of ambari when it is burning, but we have not yet heard what ambari looks like. Come on children, you only know what it is like, tell me.'

Manowari clicked his tongue with impatience, but he saw that Badfish had some plan to defeat Helandogo after they had all wrested the ambari from Haji. To humour the old man he encouraged and helped Ali and Juma to describe the size of the lump, its colour, the hardness of it, even the dent in it where the small piece that Ali had put in his pocket had fallen out of the lump.

Badfish reached into a basket and produced a coco-nut.

'Like this?' he asked.

'Yes, but rounder and with no dents like a face at one end,' said Ali.

'And no point at the other,' said Juma.

Badfish reached into the big pot of porridge and scooped up some off the top which had cooled into a fairly firm crust. He smeared and moulded the doughy stuff over the coco-nut until it was rounded over.

'Like this?' he asked.

' Yes, like that a little,' said Ali, but he held out his hand for the ball, and Badfish passed it to them.

Ali and Juma had often made little figures out of clay while they were sitting by the river at home watching their fathers' goats browsing. This was a game they understood. Between them, they patted and smoothed the dough until it seemed more like their stolen lump of ambari. Ali even fashioned the dent and then handed their work back to Badfish.

Manowari looked on, at first scornfully, but when Badfish said to Ali: ' That squid's beak—it is in your pocket?' he glanced at Badfish with growing interest. Ali rummaged about and gave the little beak to Badfish, who carefully squashed it into the bottom of the dented place, but so that it could still be seen.

Badfish turned the lump round and round, muttering first, ' Maybe,' then—' I don't know.' Then— ' We'll see.'

' You perceive a way of what sort, old one?' asked Manowari.

But Badfish would only say, ' Follow the way you have arranged with those four rogues. If you get the ambari from Haji bring it to me at once—you understand? You may get the ambari from Haji, but do you know how to prevent Helandogo and the others from getting it from us? When you give the ambari to me let Helandogo see I have it.'

Manowari looked long at Badfish and then shook his head and chuckled.

76

' I think I perceive your way, old one, but I don't perceive it clearly.'

' It is the affair of God,' said Badfish. ' Let us rest till the appointed time.'

.   .   .   .   .

Ali and Juma had hardly dozed off, it seemed to them, when they were awoken by Ishmael telling Manowari that Haji wanted everyone aft. Instead of shouting and bellowing in his usual manner, Ishmael was talking quietly, almost whispering. This seemed so peculiar to the boys that they sensed there was some mystery afoot. They sat up and looked after Manowari and saw that the rest of the crew were stumbling aft in the darkness.

Badfish said, ' Go with Manowari, children.'

' Draw near, everyone,' Haji was saying quietly as the boys caught up with Manowari, whom they found standing with Helandogo, Bullet, Bicycle and Soap in the space before the poop. The Arab members of the crew filled in the rest of the space. Their white caps and long white garments gleamed in the dark like a ghostly company. ' Now listen, every man,' Haji went on. ' Just astern you can see the light from Salim's dhow. We are just off Lamu now—that light is from the town. There is no wind to take us in. If we are to win the race for the cargo, there is only one way to be certain of getting our ship in before Salim's. We must tow this ship in with the long-boat and, to be sure of beating Salim, we must start before

Salim gets his boat out. We must launch the boat in silence so that Salim does not realize what we are doing. Even now, Salim may be thinking of the same plan or actually launching his own boat. There must be no shouting and no singing until the towing starts. You understand?'

There was a low murmur. 'We understand.'

Then a deep voice said, ' There is one small affair!'

Manowari had spoken over the heads of the crowd. Helandogo, Bullet, Bicycle and Soap faded from the back of the crowd and vanished forrard in the direction of the long-boat.

'Manowari!' exclaimed Haji impatiently. 'You want what? An affair of what sort?'

Angry exclamations came from the ghostly Arabs. Ali and Juma, standing on either side of Manowari, each clutched at a leg of his white shorts and wondered what was coming next.

'An affair of justice,' said Manowari, stoutly. 'These two children want their property.'

'What property?' asked Haji.

'Their ambari, which you took out of their canoe, said was worthless, and threw into the coil of rope up there.' Manowari pointed up to the poop. 'It is now in your big chest.'

'You fool!' said Haji. 'If I had let the children have it then do you think they would have it now? La! Either you or some other rogue would have it. The ambari will be given to the children by me in the D.C.'s office at Lamu; till then it stays where it is.

Are we to lose the cargo because of this nonsense? Ishmael, unlash the long-boat quietly and have all ready for towing.'

For a moment Ali and Juma hesitated. Was Haji really their friend after all? Then they remembered Haji's cruel eyes and clutching fingers when he had found the lump.

Ali said to Manowari, ' He is bad—completely.'

Manowari spoke up again. ' Not so! ' he said firmly and with the first sign of burning anger. ' The boat will not be unlashed until the ambari is put in my hand.'

Even in the dark it was possible to sense the fury which was tearing at Haji's heart as he asked bitingly, ' And who will prevent the unlashing? You, by yourself? '

' We black men will prevent it,' said Manowari. ' If we do not prevent it we will delay it, and Salim will get the cargo at Lamu.'

Haji drew a long hissing breath. ' Ishmael, and all of you—unlash the boat—sweep these sons of hell aside. This is mutiny. All who defy me in my ship will go to jail.'

Manowari ran to the long-boat to join Helandogo and the rest, shouting to Ali and Juma to go to Badfish in the galley. The placid contented Manowari was now mad with the excitement of battle. The threat of jail, or even death, could not reach his mind for the roaring of his hot blood in his ears.

Helandogo and his three friends had armed themselves with lengths of firewood from the cargo, and were standing between the long-boat and the stern, so that no one could get to the boat without a fight. Manowari snatched a stout stick which Helandogo had ready for him. The five Africans stood facing the crowd of white-robed Arabs, who were advancing on them with knives gleaming, Ishmael in the lead.

For a moment the two sides faced each other in silence. Then Ishmael gave a yell and sprang to the attack, followed by a shouting mass of white-robed figures. Manowari and his men gave an answering shout, sprang forward with flailing club and aimed a blow at Ishmael which pulled the mate up short. As Ishmael stopped his followers stopped too and contented themselves with screaming insults at the Africans, who advanced towards them with swift swinging blows at their ankles. A yell came from Ishmael, and the Arabs pressed forward again. The Africans were forced back and back until they were back to the long-boat, overcome by sheer weight of numbers.

The noise of shouting and yelling suddenly rose to hoarse screams of rage as a red-hot light, weaving like a giant firefly gone mad, joined in the fight. Little old Badfish had thrust a brand into his brazier until the end had burst into flame. He was now cackling and screeching as he laid about the white garments of the attackers. The Arabs fell back again.

The noise was now terrific, but was suddenly cut

short by the voice of Haji, who had appeared in front of Ishmael.

' Silence! ' he cried, in his high commanding tone. The shouts and yells died to the heavy breathing of excited men. ' Leave off this madness, or we lose the cargo—see over there! '

Haji pointed over the side. In the first glimmer of dawn Salim's ship was a dark shape. In front of it another lower, smaller shape was gliding out from it. Salim's long-boat was launched and, as Haji's panting crew watched, a yell came from Salim's mate. The men crowded into the long-boat broke into a roar as the tow-rope straightened out and they bent to their oars and paddles and burst into their rowing-song!

Haji turned to Manowari with his face ablaze with rage His right hand was held behind his back.

In an icy voice he said, ' I will give you the children's ambari—but see for how long you can keep it. You will be in jail in a few hours for this affair! Take it! '

Haji thrust out his hand, and Manowari snatched the precious lump from him. His wide eyes gazed into Haji's crafty ones unafraid.

Manowari said slowly, ' Do you not also fear jail— you who stole the ambari from the children? '

Badfish plucked at Manowari's forearm.

' Leave off words,' he said, ' and give me the lump.'

Even while this was going on the Arabs, spitting curses, had pushed past the Africans and were swarming round the long-boat. The outrigger canoe, lying beside the long-boat, was in their way. With more curses, the matting along the ship's side was slashed and torn down and the canoe was picked up bodily and thrown over into the sea. It landed with a smack in the water.

Ali darted to the side with a wild cry, jumped overboard, and, as he came to the surface, clutched at the nearest outrigger and quickly heaved himself into the canoe. He jumped to the bow and seized the mooring-rope. Juma was standing on the ship's side, in the gap broken in the matting. Ali threw the rope, Juma caught it, and tied the canoe up so that it bobbed alongside.

There was another colossal splash as the long-boat was slid, stern-first, overboard. Almost as it touched the water, a flood of men poured into it. Oars were run out, other men with paddles crouched between the rowers, and the boat was pushed out from the ship's side.

At a raucous shout from Ishmael the rowers bent forward. Ishmael filled his lungs with air and, with his eyes bulging and the veins of his neck standing out like cords, let out a short scream. The rowers heaved together on the oars, and the paddlers stabbed their paddles into the water in the first stroke of their race. To Ishmael's repeated screams the long-boat shot forward, trailing the thick tow-rope, which had been led overside from the boat's stern to the dhow's bows. A few more strokes and the long-boat was ahead of the dhow and the curving tow-rope was lifting out of the water. The tow-rope straightened with a creak and a shower of tinkling drops and the long-boat was brought up short by the dead weight of the dhow.

Ishmael steadied his men and began the opening words of the rowing-song, which would keep the labouring crew to a fast but steady rate of striking and, above all, would keep them all striking the water together.

At first the terrific, muscle-stretching effort of tugging at the dead weight of the huge dhow took every ounce of energy that each man had. Their breath was jerked out in a hiss at the end of each long pull at the oars and caught in a grunt as they bent forward and jerked back with straining arms for the next back-breaking heave. Slowly but surely the dhow began to glide slowly after the long-boat and, as the rowers began to feel the lessening strain, they found their voices. Soon Ishmael's song was taken up by them all until it swelled into a fierce rolling sound, like the roar of the pounding breakers on the reef back at Ali's and Juma's home.

In the dhow there remained only Haji, Manowari, Badfish, Helandogo and his three friends, Ali (who had scrambled back on board from the canoe), Juma and a tall slim Somali helmsman up at the tiller.

Haji was standing up in the bows watching the rowers. The pale dawn was by now lighting the scene in pale misty colours. Ahead, the white houses along the sea-front of Lamu were gleaming palely, and their reflections reached in long, pale lines

towards the dhow. Along the sea-wall there was a
bristle of masts where small fishing-boats were beached.
A few yards away, Salim's dhow, with its yard lowered
and sail hanging in loose folds, was stealing along,
slightly ahead now, thanks to his flying start in the
towing race. Haji's yard was still at the mast-head,
with the sail, which there had been no time to lower
after the fight over the long-boat, empty and lifeless.
It was still anyone's race to the mooring-buoys, black
specks on the water ahead.

The songs and shouts from the two frantically
toiling crews of the rival long-boats was now tremend-
ous. The noise and excitement which it expressed
rolled across the harbour and echoed off the houses of
the town. People began to appear and were collect-
ing in a line of white robes and black faces all along the
sea-front. In the harbour, men returning from a
night's fishing, glided in their long canoes from sea-
ward, laughing and shouting encouragement to the
toiling rowers.

A hail came from Salim. ' Salaam, Haji. First
one to moor has the first pick of the cargo. It is
agreed? '

' Salaam aleikhum, Salim—it is agreed,' answered
Haji.

Haji left the bows and strode aft, calling the
Africans, who were grouped round Badfish's kitchen,
to follow him. Below the beautifully carved, curving
beam of the poop he turned and faced them. The
Africans formed a half-circle of sullen, hang-dog

figures with arms folded and eyes glowering anywhere but at Haji.

'Now then, all of you,' began Haji in a quiet but intense tone. 'In another few minutes the Customs Officer and his men will be aboard. You know what you have done. You have refused to obey my orders on my ship, caused a fight and nearly set my ship on fire. For crimes like these the punishment of the Government is many months, perhaps years, in jail.' Haji paused and looked round the sullen faces.

At last Manowari looked up at Haji and said: 'We were fighting for justice—what would be the punishment for stealing the ambari from the children?'

Haji's eyes flashed, but he answered steadily, 'To keep the property of children safe from thieves until their voyage is over is not stealing. Can you prove that I was not going to return it?'

'That is false!' burst out Manowari hotly, but Haji's crafty eyes merely smiled as he asked again:

'Can you prove it? The Customs Officer or the D.C. will believe whom—the master of a dhow—or his crew?' Haji laughed. 'I do not fear the judgement of a court in this case.'

There was a movement as hot anger swept round the group of Africans, but, before anyone could break into a storm of angry words, Badfish stepped forward and piped up in an ingratiating voice:

'You say truly, Haji. You are a well-known and respected sea-captain, we are but your servants. You have nothing to fear from us in the court. But, if this case is brought to the courts, you have much to lose, while we have little. We are all used to the Hoteli of Kingi George, the jail. The food is not bad and the work less hard than at sea. You only will see loss. The case will take many months to be settled, and you and your ship will have to wait here until it is decided. The owners will think what when they perceive such loss? Not only this voyage but the one after will perhaps be lost. It is your affair, not mine,' continued Badfish, with deference. 'Who am I to give advice?' The little man looked down meekly.

Haji gazed at Badfish intently with a strange look. A mixture of anger and the grudging admiration of one clever rogue for another.

'This cargo we have on board now is insured,' he answered. 'I will perceive little loss. Without you scoundrels there will be a bigger share for all who are left. As for the next voyage '—Haji bit his lip, but went on firmly, ' that is the affair of God. You have brought me loss with your crimes, but I must bear the loss. Is mutiny to go unpunished? '

Badfish seemed to crumble up before Haji's righteous attitude. He looked up pleadingly into Haji's face, and his eyes were full of tears. He joined his skinny hands as if in prayer.

' We are all poor men, Haji. Our wives and children in " Haven-of-Peace " will do what while we are in jail? '

Haji laughed. ' What they always do when you are in jail,' he said.

' Ee-eh, Haji, you,' whined Badfish. ' Is there no way to melt your hardness and save us all from jail? '

Then a look of inspiration came over the little man's wrinkled face, and he gazed up at Haji with a new hope.

Haji laughed again. ' You have intelligence, old one, the ambari will save you all from jail, and even from death itself, since you will not have to kill each other for it or hang for the murders you would commit to get it. The ambari will be safe with me, to you it would bring great misfortune.'

Helandogo, Bullet, Soap and Bicycle broke into shouting, fear of jail fighting with greed of wealth in their confused minds. Manowari, on the other hand, looked strangely resigned to Badfish's bad bargain with Haji. Ali and Juma, hiding behind the broad seat of Manowari's shorts, were glancing at each other with eyes blazing with excitement. Would Badfish's wonderful acting and that awfully poor imitation of the lump of ambari bring off the little man's cunning plan?

While Helandogo and his friends were arguing, in an agony of divided councils, a hail came from the slim Somali helmsman.

' The Customs launch, Nakhoda (captain)—it comes to us first.' Then his voice rose to a triumphant shout. ' The wind, Nakhoda—and Salim's sail is down! '

Haji said quickly, ' The ambari, old one, give it to me—quickly! ' Then he turned on the rest. ' Manowari—and all of you—man the sheet and trim the sail as I order.' Badfish, who had gone off to the galley at Haji's bidding, dawdled back with a dirty old basket. Haji was in a fever of impatience. ' Hurry, hurry! ' he cried, and snatched the basket from Badfish and peered inside.

Badfish held the fish in the basket to one side so that Haji could see part of the lump, the part where the piece had fallen out and the beak of a squid had now become exposed. Haji's eyes gleamed in triumph. He dived with his prize into his own living-space under the poop.

Ali and Juma had by now skipped to the side and, as soon as Haji had disappeared, they scrambled overboard and into their canoe, which was still alongside.

Badfish tossed something to Ali and said, ' Don't forget, be at the well.' Then he cast off the mooring-rope.

By the time that Haji had hidden the fish-basket, mounted the poop, judged the direction of the gentle breath of wind, given his orders for the setting of the sail, and gone forrard to the bows to shout back his directions to the helmsman, there was one more canoe astern of the two slowly racing dhows. In that canoe, however, there were no fish, only two very young-looking fishermen. Soon the two boys had set Baba's cloth for a sail and the little grey catspaw which was creeping over the water filled the sail and sent it gliding gently, but ever more swiftly, to the line of fishing-boats grounded along the sea-front of Lamu town.

X

Friends at Lamu

ALI and Juma were heading for a solid wall of
excited people who, like a crowd on the rails of a
race-course, were cheering and shouting and dancing
up and down at the thrill of a tight finish. Behind
them was the steady roar of the two madly striving
crews.

No one seemed to notice the canoe touch gently on
the narrow beach, or see the two small boys untie the
cloth sail, stow the two long sticks in the bottom, tie
up an old baling-tin in the cloth, drag the canoe up
the beach and secure it with its mooring-rope, and
then scramble up the stone steps to the roadway, with
one of the boys clasping the cloth bundle firmly. Yet,
no sooner had Ali and Juma pushed through the
crowd, than two people came running up with glad,
amazed faces. Ali and Juma turned sharply and
faced two white boys.

'Jambo! Jambo sana! You are doing what here?'
asked the two white boys. 'We thought you had
finished dying in the sea.'

The faces of Ali and Juma lit up in recognition.
'Jambo sana—Jambo sana!' they laughed with

90

flashing teeth. Here were the two white boys with whom they had hunted for shells at home—only two days ago! 'We came in here in that dhow, the one with the sail up.'

The four boys pressed through the crowd again to see what was happening in the harbour.

Both long-boats seemed to reach their mooring-buoys together. Haji's sail and the little puff of wind had brought him up from a losing position to what seemed a dead heat. No one ashore could tell in the flurry round each buoy which had tied up first. Both crews were standing up in their boats bellowing abuse at each other and claiming to be the winners. Haji's crew pulled across to Salim's boat, and both sides started a free-for-all scrap, beating at each other with oars and clutching at each other, to fall splashing and screaming into the water. A motor boat shot out from the sea-front with a crowd of policemen in it to restore calm to the ruffled surface of the harbour.

As Ali and Juma and Peter and Andrew were laughing at the wonderful scrap the two white boys' parents pushed through the yelling onlookers.

'Look Mum!' cried Andrew. 'These two boys are safe after all—you know—the shell-boys who were swept away in the canoe.'

'I told you they'd be all right, Mum, didn't I?' said Peter.

'No, you didn't—did he, Mum?' said Andrew indignantly. 'I did, didn't I?'

'Oh, yeah?' said Peter.

' For heaven's sake shut up, you two,' said the boys' father. ' I seem to remember that each of us in turn said, " they'll be swamped," " they'll be drowned," " they'll be smashed up on the reef." We also said, " let's hope they'll be saved." Here they are anyhow,' he went on, ' alive and grinning. Let's get out of this and think what has to be done.'

The boys' mother took a handkerchief out of her bag and dabbed at her eyes.

' Their poor parents—what will they be thinking? We must tell them the good news quickly—let's go to the Post Office first.'

' It is the affair of God.' Juma grinned at Ali as they followed the white people. ' With these Europeans we are safe from Haji and Helandogo.'

' Yes,' said Ali. ' But what of Manowari and Badfish? We must meet them when they arrive out of the ship as we agreed.'

' That's it,' said Juma. ' But the Bwana can help us more than Manowari and Badfish.'

' Let us follow them now,' said Ali. ' Afterwards

we will go to the well to meet Manowari and Badfish.'

At the Post Office, Andrew and Peter's father sent a wire to the hotel near Ali's and Juma's home : ' Two boys swept out in canoe safe Lamu. Bringing them back. Please tell parents police. Masters.'

After the telegram had been sent, Mr Masters led them all to his farm-lorry and they drove a few miles out of town and then turned into the bush until they came to a large, shady tree. Under the tree was pitched a big green tent. When they had alighted, Andrew and Peter went off with Ali (still clutching his cloth bundle) and Juma to collect sticks and twigs. Mr and Mrs Masters sorted out the things they had bought in Lamu. Breakfast was soon ready, after a fire had been lit in a fire-place of stones. The Europeans had fried eggs and sausages and bread and marmalade. Ali and Juma had their usual porridge with lots of sugar and then the most delicious fruit out of a tin, followed by a bar of chocolate each.

The chocolate made the two shy African boys find their tongues.

' The chocolate you gave us at the hoteli helped us very much when we were in the sea at night,' said Ali.

' That's it, truly-truly,' said Juma. ' It was all we had to eat until Badfish gave us food.'

' Badfish!' exclaimed all the white people, laughing. ' What a name! Who is Badfish?'

Ali and Juma opened out under the influence of the

breakfast and the laughter. Soon they were telling all their adventures. The white people could not understand the boys' language well enough to understand all of it. There was a man Haji, 'A man bad completely', the master of the dhow, who had at any rate picked them up. Then, there were Manowari and Badfish, who were 'Men good completely'. Haji had stolen 'ambari', whatever that was, from the two boys. There had been a fight, and Badfish and Manowari had got back the ambari somehow.

'We understand in a small way,' said Peter doubtfully to Ali and Juma. 'But " ambari " is a thing of what kind of a sort?'

Ali looked at Juma and said something to him in a low voice.

Juma said, ' Yes, they are good.'

Then Ali said, ' That's it', and undid the bundle made out of Baba's cloth-sail.

Then he took out the old baling-tin, turned it upside down and shook out the round lump. He handed the lump to the white boys' father, and the European family looked at it in bewilderment.

' I know what it is!' exclaimed Andrew excitedly. ' Ambergris—Ambari—it must be. Let's have it, Dad.' He turned the lump over and over in his hands. ' Yes, its ambergris, and good-quality stuff too—it's brown instead of grey—hang! it's worth well over five pounds an ounce. How much do you think it weighs, Dad? Ten pounds?'

' Wow!' said Peter. ' Its price is shillingis many—

94

many—many completely,' he said to Ali and Juma, whose eyes and mouths opened wide with bewilderment.

'I suppose it *is* ambergris,' said the white boys' mother.

'How do you know all this, Andrew?' asked his father.

His family were used to Andrew's information on every subject under the sun. He was like a ceaselessly running tap, pouring out unwanted facts and figures, and usually they turned him off before their brains overflowed or burst with a flood of knowledge they did not want to be drowned in. Now, however, they turned to him and listened with an air of deference.

'I have seen ambergris in the museum in Nairobi,' Andrew said. 'There was a case there full of lumps of it of different sizes and a printed notice telling one all about it. Usually there is a squid's beak in it. People think that a squid's beak irritates the stomach of the whale and it gets coated over with some juices or some stuff which hardens and forms ambergris.'

'Yes, I've seen it too—I remember now,' said Peter. 'But the lumps in the museum were only models—not real, of course.'

'Of course they were real,' said Andrew hotly.

'No, they weren't, you ass, fancy putting real ambergris in a museum! They wouldn't, would they, Dad?' asked Peter.

'All right then, what do you bet?'

95

' A lump of ambergris—when I find one.'

' You'll get a lump of something else in a minute—do you want a sock? '

' I'm a liar—am I? '

' Oh! Do keep quiet, you two,' pleaded their mother. ' We've got to think what to do about all this.'

' Anyone would think that you chaps were still at a prep school,' said their father heavily. ' Thank heavens you'll be boarders next term. The more you're both socked the better.'

Andrew and Peter glanced at each other with a look of mutual understanding. Their parents were always butting in just when they were leading up to a good scrap.

Mr Masters turned to Ali and Juma and said, with a grave smile, ' This is your property '. He held out the ambergris. ' It is worth many, many shillingis—but there is much danger in it also if you carry it about. You want to do what? '

' We want to return to our homes,' said Juma, and Ali said:

' That's it—but there is the affair of my Baba's canoe. I can return with it how? I don't know.'

' But in this ambari there is enough money to buy many canoes,' said Mr Masters.

Ali only looked down and said obstinately, ' It is necessary that it returns—without it, I can face my father how? I can't.'

Mr Masters looked down at Ali. What he saw in

96

the half-averted face and the despondent attitude
made him grasp Ali's brown shoulder.

'Very well then, there are no more words about the
canoe. We must go to Lamu now and try to fix up
this affair.'

'It would fit in the lorry, Dad, if we took off the
outriggers,' said Peter. 'We only have the tent and
the food boxes.'

'Yes,' said Mr Masters. 'Its weight will help to
keep the wheels on the ground on the bad bits of the
road.'

'But the ambergris,' said Mrs Masters, 'we must
help them over that—what can we do?'

Mr Masters turned to Ali and Juma. 'You want
to do what with the ambari?' he asked.

Ali and Juma did not seem as interested in the
ambari as they had been in the fate of their canoe, but
at last Ali said, 'We agreed to meet Manowari and
Badfish at the well in the town when they could leave
the dhow. They told us to stay all day at the well
until they finished arriving.'

'And then what were they going to do?' asked
Mr Masters.

'We were going to cut the ambari in four pieces
and each take one piece,' said Juma. 'They helped
us much. We owe them a reward.'

'They helped you how?' asked Mr Masters.
'Explain it slowly-slowly.'

When Ali and Juma had told of the dummy lump
of ambergris, the fight for the long-boat and how

97

Badfish had palmed off the coco-nut wrapped in porridge on Haji, Mr Masters slapped his leg and laughed.

'They certainly helped you truly-truly,' he said. 'I, too, would like to meet Manowari, and especially Badfish. I wish I could see Haji too, just as he finds time to look properly at that lump of his.' He turned to his wife. 'We're letting ourselves in for something, I can tell you,' he said. 'I can see the law creeping into all this sooner or later.

'Listen, children,' Mr Masters went on. 'This is a very big affair, which I myself am unable to fix up properly. I can help you, though, to look after this ambari until we can put it in a safe place. After that we will have to talk with your fathers and decide how this ambari can be sold and turned into money. After that, we can give a proper reward to Manowari and Badfish. Do you understand?'

'We perceive,' said Ali and Juma doubtfully.

'You want me to help you?' said Mr Masters.

'That's it,' said Ali and Juma.

'Good then,' said Mr Masters. 'Let us go and find Manowari and Badfish.'

'And my father's canoe?' asked Ali.

'Yes—yes—we'll get the canoe,' said Mr Masters.

Ali and Juma clambered happily into the cab of the lorry, while Mrs Masters and her two sons stayed in the camp to look after the ambergis. In a few minutes Mr Masters had driven back into Lamu.

XI

Farewell, Haji !

MR MASTER'S first call was at the police station. Ali and Juma, in the lorry, watched him go into the building and waited patiently for him to come out again. After what they had heard from Helandogo, Bullet, Soap and Bicycle of the customs of the police, they were not very happy about this visit of Mr Masters. However, they were not the sort of boys to worry about anything that was not, at the moment, causing them any trouble.

After some time Mr Masters came out with a young and smart police-officer. The officer got into a blue truck. Two African constables got into the back of the truck. The officer waved to Mr Masters, who waved back to say he was ready, and the two moved off. The police truck led the way. Very soon both vehicles stopped in a quiet street. The officer came back to Mr Masters and said, ' The well is just round that corner. Let's stay here and send these two boys to meet their friends. You could stroll past after a bit to make sure they have met, then come back here. Perhaps you would tell the boys, if there is any trouble, to come back to us. It would be better if they did not tell their friends where we are.'

Ali and Juma set off down the street and turned the corner into a little open space in which stood a raised square of steps. At the top was the square hole of the well. On these steps, looking rather worried and cross, sat Manowari and Badfish, their bundles of possessions at their feet. Their faces became much more cheerful when they saw Ali and Juma coming towards them.

' A-haa, children,' Badfish greeted them in his cracked voice. ' You have gone where? ' Then he glanced at their empty hands and said anxiously, ' The ambari is where? I don't see it. You have done what? An affair of what kind of a sort? '

' There is no bad news,' said Juma quickly. ' We met with a European, good completely, and his lady and two children. They are our friends—we know them—they are living near our home and will take us back to-morrow.'

' That's it,' said Ali. ' They are good completely— the Bwana is going to return my Baba's canoe in his big gari.'

' But the ambari? ' asked Manowari impatiently. ' It is where? '

'The Bwana has it,' said Ali. 'He is guarding it for us so that it is not stolen by any one.'

'Like what? I don't know,' said Badfish. 'We can divide the ambari how, when the ambari is with the Bwana?'

'The Bwana says that first he will take us with the ambari to our Babas. Then we will agree about what has to be done. The Bwana says that the ambari should be turned into money and then it can be shared. You will then get your rewards for helping us.'

'A-la,' exclaimed Manowari sharply. 'And how are we to receive our money on the sea? It is true that Haji has paid us off and given us our wages, but we are people of the sea. We must get another ship. How will our share come to us now?'

'This European is where?' asked Badfish. 'We must talk with him over this affair, in order to make sure——'

He broke off suddenly and looked across the little square in which the well stood. Manowari, Ali and Juma followed his glance. There, coming towards them, with wide grins all over their faces, were Helandogo, Bullet, Bicycle and Soap.

The four laughing scoundrels came up and greeted Manowari, Badfish, Ali and Juma, shaking hands with each. Then they all squatted round. In spite of the air of reserve with which Manowari and Badfish had shaken hands and the somewhat frightened looks of Ali and Juma, it did not seem to occur to Helandogo and his friends that anyone could be anything but glad to see them.

'We have been looking for you everywhere,' said Helandogo genially, ' to tell you the latest news.'

'News of what sort?' asked Manowari.

'News of Haji,' said Helandogo, grinning like a whinnying horse.

Bicycle, Bullet and Soap started to laugh, and laughed until they had to clap their hands over their heads, slap their knees, and shake the tears out of their eyes.

'Eeeeh!' exclaimed Helandogo at last. 'That ambari of yours, Badfish, in the basket of fish—ambari of what kind of a sort?'

'Haji has discovered it then?' said Manowari.

The rogues rolled about with helpless laughter at the memory of Haji discovering that he had been done.

'That's it!' said Helandogo. 'He has finished perceiving that he has been *danganya-ed*.'

Helandogo sprang to his feet, the better to tell his story.

'When the Customs men had gone and you two had been pushed into that fishing-boat by Haji, he sent for us and told us that we also would receive our wages and go. We did not object, but after we had been given our wages we had to wait while the affair of the fight between the long-boats was fixed up between the police, Salim and Haji.

'As soon as the police and Salim had gone, Haji

went to his sleeping-place. Almost at once we heard screams from Haji. "Abu kelb—Abu kelb!" As those who understand the language of the Arabs know —those are bad words. Haji came out from below the poop with the face of Shaitani—fierce completely— like one gone mad.' Helandogo struck an attitude and bulged his eyes out, pinched in his nose and lips, and grasped an imaginary dagger to show how Haji looked in his fury.

'He had the fish-basket in his hand.' Helandogo hung down his left hand by his side. 'Then he swung this hand and the basket went flying over the side. As it hit the water—Pah! the dead fish came out, and then, what we thought was the ambari, floated out.

'We rushed to the side, ready to dive in and get it when, eh! The ambari turned into a coco-nut before our eyes! Then stuff like porridge floated away from it. We saw lots of little fish come up and they *guguna-guguna-ed*.' (Helandogo pinched his forefingers and thumbs together to show how the little fish had nibbled on the surface.) 'After we had stared at this miracle saying to each other, "Like what—like what?" we perceived how Haji had been *danganya-ed*.

'We all started to laugh and clap our hands and hold each other so that we might not fall down on the deck. Then Soap gave a shout, and we saw Haji coming towards us with his hand on his dagger, and we perceived our deaths in his eyes. There was the small boat of a man trying to sell something alongside, so we left the ship in haste and pushed the boat off by force. Haji stood at the side of the dhow. I think he had lost the power of speech. He looked at us—that was all—just looked at us.

'We all smiled and shouted "Farewell—Haji!" like men of manners, but he did not answer. He kept silent, that's all—then he went to his own place under the poop.'

Badfish was shaking his head between his knees and snickering to himself, while Helandogo was shouting and stamping and acting the wonderful drama. Manowari laughed and clapped old Badfish on his skinny shoulders. 'Eeeeh—you! You're like what? I don't know!'

'And now,' said Helandogo, 'we are rejoiced exceedingly that we black men have *danganya-ed* the Arabs and have recovered our property.' His voice had taken on the tone of one addressing a meeting of importance. 'I call upon Mr Badfish, Mr Manowari and these two good children to show us our ambari in order that we may divide it between us and in this manner follow the way of justice.'

'That's it!' agreed Bicycle, Soap and Bullet genially, but there was an underlying note in their voices that made Ali and Juma draw closer to Manowari and caused Badfish to look round at the rogues with pursed mouth and screwed-up eyes.

Helandogo glanced in turn at Manowari, Badfish, Ali and Juma. Not one of them had anything in his hands. There was nowhere else about any of them where the ambergris could be concealed. His face

became set, and his eyes began to stick out from the pressure of the thought behind them.

'The ambari—it is where?' he asked, fiercely and intensely. 'Speak!'

Soap, Bicycle and Bullet sprang up and faced the others, still sitting on the steps of the well.

'Answer,' they shouted menacingly. 'It is where—speak—that's all!'

Manowari raised his calm eyes to their enraged ones and said, 'The ambari is the property of the children. As for me, I do not know where it is, neither does the old one.'

'Truly-truly I myself know not,' said Badfish.

Helandogo turned to Ali and Juma, and as he did so Manowari stood up unhurriedly but purposefully to defend them if need be.

'Leave the children alone,' Manowari said in a level voice. 'Even if they tell you where it is you cannot get it. It has been left with one who would not give it to anyone but the fathers of these children. Right then! You can do what?'

Helandogo and his friends broke into screams of rage.

'Liars!' they yelled. 'Give us our shares!'

'For doing what?' cried Manowari. 'Trying to steal it from the children and failing? Go away, you thieves!'

'Leave off idle words,' screamed Badfish. 'Profit of what kind of a sort comes from fighting for something that cannot be seized?'

Then his jaw dropped and his eyes became fixed. Even in their excitement the dazed look in the little man's face made the rest stop and follow his gaze.

Helandogo and his friends gave one glance—then panic seized them and, as one man, they bolted for a narrow alley-way and disappeared. In half an hour or so they would be laughing and singing, buying trash in the shops and beer in dark and sinister houses with their hard-won shillings. They had tried and failed to get something which was not theirs—well then—that affair was over—finish!

Ali and Juma clutched even more firmly at Manowari's shorts, and Badfish stood like a frog before a snake. Haji, in his spotless white shore-going garments, his beautiful dagger in his belt and an ebony walking-stick in his hand, was striding towards them, followed by Ishmael.

Manowari drew himself up—stood to attention—and faced Haji with his chin up and eyes level. Ali and Juma were still clutching Manowari's shorts. Badfish still gazed, as if fascinated by terror, at Haji's stately and relentless approach; his face held a greyish tinge of fear. Badfish, however, had still something of courage left in him. As Haji came closer Badfish screwed his wizened face into a ghastly grin, raised his two hands to the sides of his face and greeted his old captain bravely.

'Jambo sana, Nakhoda!—Jambo!'

Manowari also saluted, Navy-fashion. 'Jambo, Nakhoda!'

Haji stopped a few paces from them. He looked past Manowari and fixed his blazing black eyes on Badfish.

'Son of a Dog!' he said with a deadly intensity. 'Give me that ambari—thief!'

'Ah! Haji—I myself am no——'

'The ambari is where?' Haji spat out.

Manowari answered him. 'It is in a place of safety. Neither the Old One nor myself knows where it is truly-truly. Only those know whose property it is.'

'The children—eh?' Haji's eyes fixed themselves on Ali's right eye and Juma's left eye—the only eyes he could see; the other two were hidden by Manowari's shorts. 'Come out here and stand in front of me,' Haji ordered. Ali and Juma reluctantly came out from behind Manowari. 'Now then,' Haji said, 'where is the ambari?' Ali and Juma looked down and wriggled their toes in discomfort. 'Come on— speak up,' said Haji, 'or I report your friend Manowari to the police for the mutiny in my ship, and Badfish for trying to set fire to it. I will count up to thirty; if you have not started to tell me by then— finish! I will go straight to the police.'

. . . .

Ali and Juma had left home only two days ago as happy boys who had seen nothing of life and people outside their own village. They were shy and awkward with strangers, and only at ease with those they knew well. They could be cheeky occasionally to their parents or to old Mwalimu, their school-teacher, but with strangers they were tongue-tied.

In their two crowded days and nights of adventure they had borne themselves well, but had neither said nor done anything of note. Things had happened to them, but they had not made anything happen by their own courage, brains or determination. They had not lost their shyness.

As they stood in front of Haji, with his burning eyes fixed on them, knowing that he was counting thirty to himself before trying to avenge himself on their two friends, the two boys found a strange feeling surging up inside themselves.

Ali felt as he did in his dream. The strength to fight the bully Squidface, which had filled him just as Joogoo, the cock, had woken him by his trumpet-call, filled him now. There was a longing also to be cheeky. He had to give lip to Haji—but wait—there was something better than cheek to dish out to Haji! Ali suddenly looked up and met Haji's eyes squarely.

' Leave off this affair of counting inside your head,' said Ali, ' and follow me.'

Juma also found his tongue, as his own heart became inspired with the idea of giving Haji a bit of lip.

' That's it,' he piped up, and he, too, looked fearlessly in Haji's eyes. ' Profit of what kind of a sort comes from standing there and beating out a count in your bongo? '

From that moment Ali and Juma were able to speak up and look at people without wriggling their toes and hanging their heads. They had twisted something that was happening to them into something that they wanted to happen their way. Not every African boy can stand up to an Arab sea-captain and order him to follow.

. . . . .

' Lead on—children of Satan,' said Haji, with a gleam in his eye that might have been appreciation. ' Ishmael, see that these two mjinga's do not run away.'

' Do not fear, Haji, we will not run,' chuckled Manowari.

Badfish clutched his mouth with his right hand and snickered furtively into it.

Ali and Juma strode out with purposefully swinging arms and some importance away from the well and towards the corner of the building by which they had come to meet Manowari and Badfish. As they turned the corner they increased their pace and Mr Masters and the police-officer left the side of the police truck, against which they had been leaning and came to meet them. As they met, the two boys turned round to face the four who were following them.

As soon as Haji rounded the corner and saw the two boys with the two Europeans, one of them a police-officer, he came to an abrupt halt. The rest stopped behind him. Manowari nudged Badfish and they both pushed past in front of Haji and Ishmael.

Haji's pause was only for a moment. He recovered himself at once and, with Ishmael following, came forward—the perfect picture of the dignified Arab gentleman, successful master-mariner and merchant-adventurer that, indeed, he was. He greeted the police-officer with friendliness and dignity.

' Ah! Haji—Salaam aleikhum! ' said the officer. ' You are having trouble of some sort? '

' No trouble, Effendi—thank you,' said Haji in a friendly voice. ' I have been worried about these two children.' He waved a graceful hand at Ali and Juma. ' I picked them up in their canoe off Strife and wished to take them to you to make a report when I arrived. They are not children of much intelligence, and disappeared from my ship this morning in their canoe. I am glad to see they have come to you at last and are now in safe hands.'

Haji saluted Mr Masters and the police-officer.

' Yes,' said the officer to Haji. ' This gentleman has offered to take them back to their homes near " In-the-deep-waters " with their canoe, so *all* their property will be safe.' He looked hard at Haji, but Haji was too tough an old bird to flicker an eyelid.

An expression of relief came over his face. ' Allah be praised,' he said. ' You have set my mind at rest over these two children.'

' Is there any other affair? ' asked the officer.

' Many thanks, Effendi,' replied Haji. ' There is

nothing. At least '—he eyed Manowari and Badfish
—' nothing I cannot manage myself. I wish only to
speak to these two men from my ship. They have not
pleased me and I have discharged them, but there is
something I would like to say to them now.'

' You wish to bring any charge against them? '
asked the officer.

' No, no, Effendi, it is just a small affair,' said Haji;
then, turning to Manowari and Badfish, ' Come here,
you two.' Haji drew Manowari and Badfish a little
way away and said to them in a low voice, ' Do not
try and obtain work in a ship belonging to any one of
my friends, you will not get work, you understand? '

Manowari and Badfish both acted as if Haji had
paid them some nice compliment. Each gave Haji a
broad grin and said loudly, ' Good Haji, we hear, good
completely, Eeeh! That's it—farewell, now.' They
rejoined Ali and Juma.

Haji saluted the police-officer and Mr Masters with
a courteous smile. He turned without even glancing
at any of the Africans and, followed by Ishmael,
walked in stately and unhurried fashion down the
street.

It was not until Haji was out of sight and ear shot
that the police-officer laughed and said, in a tone of
admiration:

' The old scoundrel! '

' He may be an old scoundrel—but he's a well-bred
one,' said Mr Masters.

' He's got the nerve of the devil. He hardly ever

comes in here without some sort of funny business cropping up,' said the police-officer. ' The Customs people have been waiting for years to catch him. Only after he has finished a voyage we hear rumours of smuggling or something. He's probably got some elephants' tusks even now in his ballast if we only knew it. He's a first-class sailor, anyhow. Ah, well— I'll be getting back to the office to see what's cropped up in my absence. Good-bye! '

' Good-bye to you,' said Mr. Masters. ' And many thanks for the help.'

When the police truck had gone, Mr Masters turned to Manowari and Badfish.

' Let us go first to get the children's canoe,' he said. ' After that we can go to my camp and we can talk about this affair—you agree? '

' Good then, Bwana, we agree,' said Manowari and Badfish in turn.

At the steps on the sea-front the lorry was halted. Ali and Juma ran down and found their canoe just as they had left it. Mr Masters measured it and then the back of his lorry with his arms and decided that it would fit, but only if they took off the outriggers. Ali did not like this (' My father will say what? I don't know '), but Manowari soon persuaded him that a dismantled canoe was better than none at all.

The lashings of the outriggers were cut with Mr Masters' penknife, and the sticks and boards from which they were made were carefully stowed in the canoe. The sight of a European working at a canoe had collected a small crowd, and some of them were roped in by Manowari to help. The canoe was hoisted up the steps and then into the back of the lorry. The stern stuck out of the back, so that the tailboard of the lorry could not be closed, but otherwise there was no trouble. Mr Masters doled out his small change to the helpers and drove off hurriedly before all the loafers in the town could appear, like vultures, to claim something they had never earned.

Before leaving the town, Mr Masters bought food for Manowari and Badfish, while Ali and Juma joyfully sat in the back of the lorry guarding the canoe. Then they set off for the camp in the bush.

XII

We will do What?

FROM what he had seen of Manowari and Badfish, Mr Masters had to decide whether to trust them or not. The little old man seemed a bit of a character, certainly not evil in any way. Manowari was a fine-looking chap; smart, clean, held himself in a well-disciplined way, had an open, frank way of speaking and steadfast eyes. How much had these two really helped the two boys for their own sake—and how much for what they could get out of their ambergris? Supposing Andrew and Peter had not seen Ali and Juma when the African boys had landed at Lamu and Ali and Juma had been left on their own, what would have happened to them and their ambergris?

Mr Masters, driving his lorry and asking himself these questions, glanced at the little man by his side and at the big sailor at the other end of the seat. He had been long enough in East Africa to know that he had made many mistakes in trying to judge Africans.

He had given up trying, and now merely acted towards them as if they were to be trusted until they themselves showed whether they were trustworthy or not. He felt that Ali and Juma might have met two very much worse friends than Manowari and Badfish. He would just have to wait and see.

When they arrived in the camp under the big mango-tree, Mr Masters' family did not seem to have doubts about Manowari and Badfish as he had. It was nearly lunch-time, and Badfish was drawn irresistibly to the fire, where Mrs Masters was cooking. In no time, Badfish had taken over what was to him just another ' galley,' and Mrs Masters found herself laying the table in the welcome coolness away from its heat.

Andrew and Peter were attracted by the strength and capable air of Manowari. They clambered with him into the back of the lorry, where Ali and Juma still were, to see how the canoe had stood up to the short but bumpy journey.

Before his family gathered for lunch, Mr Masters said to Manowari and Badfish, ' These two children, Ali and Juma, wish to reward you for helping them over the affair of the ambari—you yourselves think what? '

' It is a big affair, Bwana,' said Badfish. ' The children can settle it how? It is an affair for their fathers and the old ones of their village to decide.'

' That's it, Bwana,' said Manowari. ' I can see one difficulty only.'

' A difficulty of what sort? ' asked Mr Masters.

' This old one and I,' said Manowari, ' are people of the sea. Haji pushed us out of our ship for what we did to help the children. It will be difficult indeed for us to find another ship in Lamu now. Haji will tell the other dhow-masters that we are bad—finish! We can do what? '

Mr Masters thought for awhile, then he said, ' You cannot get work in Lamu, but in Strife or in " In-the-deep-waters " the Nakhodas do not know what Haji is saying about you. I can take you there with Ali and Juma.'

The faces of Manowari and Badfish broke into smiles.

' Good, Bwana, good completely! '

And Badfish added, ' And again, by this road we can meet the fathers of the children and fix up the affair of our reward.'

' Well then,' said Mr Masters. ' To-morrow, very early, we start our journey back. To-night we will talk some more.'

He gave Manowari and Badfish the food he had bought for them, and they carried it off to a neigh-bouring tree and, with Ali and Juma, cooked a meal of their own out of sight of the European family.

After lunch, Badfish firmly established himself as cook to the Masters, while Manowari, Andrew, Peter, Ali and Juma went wandering off into the bush. Andrew and Peter carried their .22 rifles, in the hope of shooting something for the pot. The few guineafowl and partridge-like spur-fowl they saw were too wily for them, and they returned empty handed, except for Manowari, who carried the big branch of a dead tree on his shoulders.

In the evening, after supper, Manowari's branch became a clear leaping flame in the camp-fire. Mr Masters invited him and Badfish, Ali and Juma, to sit in its brightness while they discussed what was to be done.

Within the circle of light cast by the fire was the low rushing noise made by the flames and the murmur of human voices. Outside, were the noises of the African night. Somewhere near there was a stream or marshy place from which came the continuous voices of hundreds of frogs. It was as if an army of dwarfs were busy in some vast factory, beating out musical instruments of every kind by the score. The noise of their hammers made a continuous clamour. All around, in the grass and bushes, thousands of insects were vibrating their bodies, to produce a steady, high-pitched note that seemed to sing in the human brain. Against this background of strident energy the human conversation proceeded.

'It is difficult to speak much more about this affair,' Mr Masters was saying, 'until we meet the fathers of Ali and Juma, but we can discuss what is to be done before we arrive at their homes. You think we should do what?' he asked.

Badfish gave his little cackling laugh. 'We are people of the sea, Bwana. I know how to catch fish and to cook. Manowari is an expert completely in steering a ship along the ways of the sea—but for an affair of business—we know what ? '

' Not one thing—even-in-a-small-way,' said Manowari. ' But you are a European—you are as our father in this affair.'

Mr Masters sighed. ' If you had not met me or some other European, you would have done what ? ' he asked.

' We had agreed to share the ambari with the two children by splitting it,' said Badfish. ' Then the children met you. It was the affair of God, that's all.'

' But if you had not met me ? ' persisted Mr Masters. This appeared to be a stupid question to Manowari and Badfish, since it was about something that had not happened.

At last, Badfish said, with a laugh, ' Each of us would have tried to sell his piece of ambari to an Arab or an Indian. Well then—we do not know the price of ambari—we would have been *danganya-ed* completely. We would have got a little money—finish ! '

' There is a question, Bwana,' said Manowari. ' This ambari of the children—its value is shillingis how many ? '

' I don't know,' said Mr Masters, who turned to Andrew. ' What do you remember about the price of it per pound ? You said you saw it in the museum in Nairobi.'

' It depends on the quality,' said Andrew, ' but the

lowest is five pounds per ounce. A better quality is much more valuable.'

'We cannot say.' Mr Masters turned again to the Africans. 'But it is several hundreds of shillingis. We can only wait until we get to Strife, there I can find out from the people of the Customs who can value ambari and how it can be sold. In this way we can tell the fathers of Ali and Juma when we get to their homes.'

'Many hundreds of shillingis!' exclaimed Manowari. 'The children's Babas will rejoice exceedingly. Afterwards, they will do what? They will be men of wealth!'

Mr Masters smiled at the two African boys. 'Ali,' he said. 'Your father will do what?'

Ali appeared to be thinking deeply. 'I don't know,' he said at last. 'It will be his own affair.'

'And Juma, your father will do what?'

'He'll *pumzika* (rest)—that's all!' said Juma promptly.

This made the Masters family laugh, and Ali, encouraged to say more and to out-do Juma, said:

'My Baba will buy more goats and some clothes, *maridadi* completely!'

Then Ali, to go one better than Juma, said, 'My father will buy a field and sell vegetables'.

Juma said, 'Mine will buy a shop and sell things— food of every kind, sweets, *maridadi* clothes and many other beautiful things.'

His eyes shone with excitement as his imagination,

aroused at last, began to show him what the ambari could bring.

Badfish broke in. 'Ah! child, you know what? Your father is a fisherman—not so? You think a fisherman has the ability to run a shop like an Arab or an Indian? No! He would only perceive a great loss after a little and lose all his property.'

'Well then, Old One,' said Mr Masters, smiling. 'You yourself think what?'

Badfish paused and gazed into the fire, scratched his grey head and at last faced Mr Masters.

'Bwana,' he said, 'I have seen many black people get some money all of a sudden. I have not seen one who did not lose it again, almost as quickly. Some have *pumzika-ed* completely until it was all gone and then returned to work. Some have spent it all on drink and afterwards have not had the heart to work. Some have bought goats or land and have seen but little profit. Some have started little shops, but their own people have come each day to get something for nothing, for are they not relations? In one month or two—finish—the shop is dead. We black people know only one road with money, truly-truly. We are experts completely at spending it all without profit.'

The little old man shook his head sadly and chuckled at human folly.

'Bwana,' said Manowari, 'the Old One has spoken truly-truly. Now I ask you. You yourself would do what in this affair if you were the father of one of these children?'

' I am a white man,' said Mr Masters. ' I cannot understand exactly what a black man would want to do with his money. And yet,' he went on, ' we are all sons of Adam and want the same sort of things. These children's fathers will want to help them, is it not so? '

' That's it! ' said Manowari eagerly. ' You are going to say by paying for good education, then they can become clerks, men of intelligence? '

' No,' said Mr Masters. ' Education is good certainly, but there are too many clerks already. If the children are very good at learning in school, good, they may be able to get work as clerks, but if they cannot get good reports from school they will do what? They will just wander about looking for work as clerks. They will not get it because their reports will not be good enough. Work with their hands they will not do because they will have learnt to despise it.'

' Truly-truly,' said Badfish, ' the country is full of men who call themselves clerks. There is no work for them, so they *tanga-tanga* about, good for nothing completely.'

' You, Ali—and you, Juma—you like school? ' asked Mr Masters.

' *Not* at all! ' said Ali and Juma cheerfully, and Andrew and Peter laughed sympathetically.

' We want to fish, that's all,' said Ali.

' That's it,' said Juma.

' The money from the ambari,' said Mr Masters, ' it can help a fisherman in what way? I do not know much about the business of fishing. I am a stranger to the coast.'

'My father is a fisherman,' said Manowari. 'A fisherman needs little; a canoe—nets—traps, also, if he can get one, an *uzio*' (a fence of sticks set up in shallow water with a trap at one end into which the fish can be driven and then caught).

Ali glanced towards the lorry at the mention of 'canoe.'

'My father has all these things—except the *uzio*—and all we people in the village share one in the water beyond the headland,' he said. 'My Mama makes the nets, but the canoe has to be bought. My Baba even now is paying to the canoe-maker each month a little and a little until it is paid for.'

'Well then,' asked Mr Masters. 'The money from the ambari can help in what way? The best thing to do with money is to make it produce more money—like a cow or a sheep.'

Mrs Masters asked suddenly, 'How do they make a profit from their fish?' She turned to Manowari. 'Your father does what with the fish he catches?' she asked.

Manowari answered, 'My mother takes all the fish to the market and there she stands all day trying to sell them. All the other women of the village are there too. The profit is small, but it suffices for two old people like my father and mother—they do not perceive hunger. When I come home, after a voyage, I give them some of my wages to help them.'

'There is one little difficulty with fish,' said Bad-fish. He chuckled. 'My parents also lived by fish. On the day that I was born my father must have perceived that difficulty. Maybe he had a good catch that day and my mother could not go to market —finish!—bad fish!'

After the burst of laughter had died down Mrs Masters leant forward eagerly in her chair.

'I believe I have an idea,' she exclaimed. 'You remember the day we went exploring down to " Place-of-the-cave "? A Company has been formed which has a refrigerating-plant there. The fishermen bring in their catch and sell it to the Company—cash down, I think—then the fish are frozen and sent to Strife by lorry. All the fishermen have to do is catch fish and they have a certain market, no worries about bad fish ' (she laughed at the little old man) ' when their wives cannot get about.'

'Yes,' said Mr Masters, ' but Ali and Juma live too far from " Place-of-the-cave " to take their fish—— Oh! You mean transport?' he said to his wife.

'I know,' said Peter, ' a motor boat—it is not nearly as far to " Place-of-the-cave " by sea as it is by land. The road winds about round those creeks and inlets.'

'I was thinking of a van,' said Mrs Masters, ' but I believe a motor boat would be better.'

'It's a good idea,' said Mr Masters. ' The trouble is we know so little about the price of ambari, the price of a motor boat and about fishing. At any rate this idea of yours seems the only sort of thing that would fit into the normal lives of these people! '

Mr Masters turned to Manowari, Badfish, Ali and Juma and explained what they had been saying. ' It is only what we thought, we do not know what profit it would bring,' he ended.

Manowari and Badfish were enthusiastic. They laughed at each other and shook their heads, clapped one hand into another and said, ' Eh!—Europeans!— I don't know!—Intelligence!—Ah! '

Then Manowari said cheerfully, ' Do not perceive doubt over the profit, Bwana. The boat with the *tinga-tinga* can be used to carry the fish of all the people in the village. It can be full of fish. The fathers of the children can charge the people a-little a-little for taking their fish to the Company at " Place-of-the-cave " and for returning with their money.'

' Hang! What fun! ' said Peter enviously. He turned to Ali and Juma and said in their language, ' To-morrow year we will return to the hoteli near your home. We can go with you in your boat of the *tinga-tinga?* '

Ali and Juma had never said, and would never say the words ' Thank you ' to the Masters family, but they seemed to say much more when they looked at Andrew and Peter and said, ' You will come—that's all—every day.'

There was a pause in the talk, and the double chorus of frogs and insects seemed to rush in to fill its place.

Andrew drove the noise out of their brains again. 'I know where they can get a motor boat—just the thing,' he said. 'There is one for sale in the Palm Trees Hotel—you know—where the Winters are staying. The owner of the hotel is selling it because people seem to be scared of being sea-sick, or something, and won't go for trips along the coast. Mike Winter says it's as good as new.'

'Well—there we are!' laughed Mr Masters. 'The boys' fathers are practically millionaires before we've even met them.'

Manowari spoke hesitatingly. 'As for me, I rejoice exceedingly that we have been able to help the children with our words—but—now I perceive bitterness a little.'

'For why?' asked Mr Masters.

Manowari answered, 'The elders of the village will decide on a reward for me and Badfish—then we will go with our money—but we will do what with it to make it bring a profit? How can a *rubani* (helmsman) steer his money into ways of profit while he is holding the tiller of a ship all day and night?'

Ali jumped up in his excitement. 'I myself know!' he cried. 'My Baba knows what about a *tinga-tinga* boat? Not-a-thing-even-in-a-small-way!'

'My Baba same-same,' said Juma.

'Finish!' cried Ali. 'You only will steer it!'

Manowari's face lit up. He smacked his leg with a huge hand.

'It was my work in the Navy during the war,'

he said, 'to steer a motor boat in "In-the-deep-waters".'

'You have said well indeed, Ali,' said Mr Masters. He turned to Manowari and Badfish. 'When you meet the boy's fathers you can measure their hearts and see whether you can be friends with them; if you can agree together perhaps you can do this: leave off the affair of a reward in money, which would not be much for you and would take money from them. Work with the fathers in the *tinga-tinga* boat; then make an agreement to share in the profit.' Mr Masters glanced at Badfish. 'You also understand this work,' he said, 'your hair is white a little, but you still have strength and intelligence. You think what?'

The little man smiled. '"Work is profit",' he quoted. 'Will the fathers agree? I don't know. It is the affair of God.'

Mrs Masters smiled at Ali and Juma. 'You will have to work hard at school now,' she said. The two stared at her in horror, and Andrew and Peter blushed for their mother.

'Why, Mum?' asked Peter.

'Who will do the accounts and write up the books?' asked Mrs Masters in reply, speaking in the Africans' language. 'A business can progress how without clerks? You will bring in some clerk from Strife at shillingis many per month to eat your profit?'

'*Not*—at all,' Ali and Juma said together. They sat with screwed-up faces for a moment or two.

At last Ali spoke seriously. 'We'll do it—that's all.'

'That's it,' said Juma. 'I am unable to refuse.'

At that moment something seemed to snap in the universe. It was a moment before they realized what had happened. The thousands of insects had stopped their shrill symphony, as if cut off by a master-switch, and the sudden silence was startling, almost painful. Only one small insect voice was heard, chirping and trilling, presumably telling the multitude of musicians in the vast orchestra the details of the programme for to-morrow night.

The party stood up and, with many a '*Kwa heri*' (with happiness), they went off to their camp-beds or to their blankets on the ground in readiness for an early start in the morning.

XIII

Ali and Juma at Home Again

THERE was not much of the journey left. Mr Masters stopped the lorry in the big island town of Strife. After some time he came back, having deposited the ambergris with a business friend who had a safe. He went then off to the Customs Office and came back with a pleased expression on his face.

The lorry had got on to the island by a narrow toll bridge near the old dhow-harbour; it left it again by a ferry across the deep channel leading to the modern port of "In-the-deep-waters". As soon as the front wheels touched the ramp of the ferry on the far side of the channel Ali's and Juma's excitement began to grow. Ali and Manowari hung round the back of the lorry on one side and Juma and Badfish round the other. The two boys kept looking out for landmarks which would tell them when they were nearing home.

It was late afternoon when they rumbled over a bridge and saw the pool below it where they had so often bathed and splashed. They saw some of their school-friends bathing down there now. Ali and Juma yelled. The glistening brown, frog-like creatures in the stream yelled back in recognition, dashed out of the water, snatched up their scanty garments and ran naked and cheering after the home-comers.

The corrugated-iron roof of the school came into sight at last. The lorry slowed down, and the pursuing naked boys caught up. Their shouts and cheers drew people from every house in the village.

Mr Masters saw two men standing with their wives by the side of the road. Peter and Andrew recognized one of the men as Baba. Mr Masters pulled up the lorry so that the tail-board stopped by Ali's and Juma's parents, who had been waiting by the roadside all day, peering into every car that passed, waiting for this moment.

Ali looked down into the shining eyes of his father.

'I have finished returning, TOGETHER WITH THE CANOE, Baba-mine,' he shouted above the cheers and high shrilling cries of the women.

For the whole long journey from Lamu, Ali had been worried whether he could tell Baba about the canoe before Baba started asking him about it. Baba glanced at the canoe, as if it was nothing, and his eyes returned to his son.

'What news of you—you are complete—Ali you?'

'Complete, that's all!'

Mama was swaying backwards and forwards, clapping her hands, laughing and crying at the same time.

Juma jumped down, and Rajab, his father, gave him a playful cuff, saying, ' Eh! you, Juma, you're like what? I don't know! '

Juma's mother was laughing down at him fondly. ' Eh! Juma, you—you have been where? '

The Masters family had by now climbed out of the cab of the lorry and were watching the exciting scene. At last Mr Masters pushed through the packed crowd of shouting people, and gradually Ali's and Juma's parents became aware that this was the Bwana who had brought their sons back home.

Each father in turn grasped his hand in both of his and said, ' Jambo sana Bwana—we rejoice exceedingly because of you.'

Mr Masters laughed and replied, ' I also rejoice that your children have returned safely.' He then pointed up at Manowari and Badfish, who were grinning down from the lorry, enjoying the excitement. ' Those two men have helped your children very much. They are strangers, but soon you will perceive that they are very good friends. You can help them with a place to sleep? They have much to tell you. A big affair of good luck for all of you.'

Baba and Rajab held up their hands to Manowari and Badfish and made motions of scraping them towards them. ' Hiya! Come down,' they cried, ' so that we may welcome you—come down.'

Mr Masters broke in again and said to Baba,

'Your house is where? I will drive the lorry to it, and we will take off the canoe.'

Ali heard and pointed under the big mango-tree. 'There, Bwana, where those two cocks are fighting.' He ran off with Juma to separate Joogoo and Juma's cock. As he ran, Mbwa, the little yellow dog, came rushing up and jumped around him with joy.

The lorry drove across the open space, and every one in the village formed a dancing, singing procession behind it. In front of Baba's house the canoe was slid out on to the grass by willing hands, followed by Manowari's and Badfish's bundles and their food.

Mrs Masters climbed up into the lorry and rummaged about in the big box which was her camping store-cupboard. She came out again with a nearly full packet of tea and a bag of sugar, which she gave to Ali's and Juma's delighted mothers.

Mr Masters turned to Baba and Rajab. 'Now we are going to our hotel. Your two guests, Manowari and Badfish, have much to tell you—you will be astonished completely at their news. To-morrow, when you have heard everything, you will want to talk with me. When you are ready you will find me at the hotel.'

'Good completely,' said the two smiling fathers.

'*Kwa heri,*' said Mr Masters.

'*Kwa heri,* Bwana,' said Baba and Rajab.

'*Kwa heri,* Bwana,' said Manowari and Badfish.

'*Kwa heri, Kwa heri,*' chorused the crowd.

As the lorry drove back on to the road, it was

followed again by the dancing procession. At the road the crowd stopped following it, but continued dancing and singing while the drummers and musicians rushed off to get their instruments.

The dancers formed a big circle near the spreading mango-tree. The drums and the voices and the shuffling feet soon found a common rhythm. Darkness came down, the crescent moon sank below the trees, the myriad stars filled the velvet-black sky. Round and round went the circle of dancers, the sound of singing rose and fell, bare feet moved in an intricate pattern and the drums throbbed and pulsed.

Ali and Juma, shoulder to shoulder, swayed and surged round with the rest. In the centre of the circle Mwalimu, their school-teacher, was conducting the dance and maintaining order. Someone pushed in between Ali and Juma—a youth a bit taller than they. After a few more steps had been made, Ali's foot was stamped on by this youth, who, at the same time, jabbed Juma in the ribs with his elbow. The two friends turned inwards to this youth—Squidface!

Poor Squidface! He did not realize that travel broadens the mind. Before he knew what had happened he was on his back in the dust, just outside the circle of dancers, with the two returned travellers almost quarrelling for the best seat on his body, his chest, for pummelling his unlovely face. Ali settled down on the chest to avenge a hundred bullyings, leaving Juma to content himself with kicking Squidface in the ribs with his bare feet. Squidface let out a pitiful cry. A quicker surge in the dance than usual made the revolving circle swing outwards, and several people, with indignant shouts, tripped and fell in a struggling heap over Squidface's writhing legs.

Mwalimu, walking-stick in hand, came on the scene with a shout of 'An affair of what sort?' The three struggling boys were hauled to their feet by

Mwalimu, who demanded, 'Doing what?'

'This one stamped on my foot,' said Ali.

'He himself hit me in the ribs,' said Juma.

'Who?—me? Ah! Liars!' squealed Squidface. 'It was they who did that to me.' Squidface let out a swinger with his right at Ali, and thereby lost any sympathy Mwalimu might have had for him.

Mwalimu gave Squidface a swinger for himself and then said heavily, 'For why do you bring confusion into the dance? Are you unable to perceive shame? Everyone wants to rejoice completely, and the whole dance is destroyed by you introducing war. Like what?' He turned on Squidface. 'Get out, you! Return to your home—go!'

Squidface slunk off. Mwalimu turned on Ali and Juma to lecture them a bit more—because he intended to let them return to the dance; but Ali spoke up.

'There is a small affair, Mwalimu.'

'Heh? An affair of what sort?'

'An affair of education,' said Ali.

'All of you two wish to talk of education?' asked Mwalimu, in astonishment. 'For why? I have been able to teach you what?'

'Not a thing, even-in-a-small-way,' said Juma promptly, and with a certain pride. 'It is for that reason that we are talking about education now.'

'That's it,' said Ali. 'It is necessary for us to learn how to read and write.'

'*Not* at all,' said Juma. 'Leave off reading and writing—teach us how to beat a count—to take away —to cause to increase—to share out—work of figures, that's all. There is profit of what kind of a sort in reading and writing?'

'A-la!' exclaimed Mwalimu. 'All of you two are like what? Before you left here to lose yourselves in the sea, you were the most idle ones in the school— to surpass all. Now, you wish to learn the work of figures. We start now, in the middle of the night? You will circulate-circulate in the dance while I teach you the work of figures?'

'*Not* at all,' said Ali, solemnly. 'There is no opportunity just now.'

'But there is need of hurry,' said Juma. 'In about a week from now it is necessary that we have the capability of understanding the work of figures completely. After that—finish! We can leave off the work of education and seek profit in fish.'

'You have finished your intelligence completely, or like what?' asked Mwalimu, after a stunned silence. 'For why do you bother me with these words of fools?'

'Because we are men of immense wealth completely,' said Ali simply. 'And for this reason is it necessary for us to have the capability of understanding figures.'

'You are miserable tiny children with heads swollen up near to bursting. Arrive in front of me to-morrow—and look out—that's all.' Mwalimu raised his walking-stick threateningly, and his spectacles flashed in the starlight. 'Go on—get out—before I perceive anger completely.'

Mwalimu strode back to the dance, which was still going on and on to the throbbing of the drums, without any need for his presence. He pushed his way into the centre of the slowly revolving circle and redoubled his unnecessary shouts and admonitions to the happy villagers to make up for the time wasted on those nasty little boys and to re-assert his authority.

Ali and Juma ran off laughing into the dark.

'Squidface has gone where?' asked Ali. 'Let's go and beat him up again, but in secret this time.'

'I think he has run off to his house,' said Juma, 'but I saw his father and mother at the dance—he will have locked himself inside.'

'It doesn't matter,' said Ali. 'We'll get him out—follow my words when we get to his door.'

Ali banged on Squidface's door. 'Come out you, Squidface,' he called.

'Go away,' cried Squidface.

'Come out at once—or we burn your house down, and you inside,' said Ali.

'Get out,' cried Squidface again.

'All right,' said Ali. 'It's your affair, that's all—

don't abuse us when the fire starts to eat you. Hey! Juma, you,' he went on, ' give me those matches—you are with them? '

'I am with them,' said Juma, playing up. ' Here, take them—burn the grass of the roof, it will burn well.'

They heard a quick fumbling at the door and had just time to spring round the door of the hut before Squidface rushed out and stood peering round in the faint starlight. Ali and Juma sprang on him together, and once more the three boys were writhing, with flailing arms and legs, in the dust.

Unfortunately for Ali and Juma, Squidface's dog rushed out, scattering hens in every direction, and, attacking them in the rear with nips from his sharp teeth, sent them scampering off towards their own homes, pursued by jeers and insults from Squidface.

' We'll beat him yet! ' said Ali, furiously, rubbing the seat of his pants.

' That's it,' said Juma. ' When teachers and dogs are not present to protect him.' He stopped to wipe some blood off a small tooth-mark in the calf of his leg. ' We will make a custom of beating him up completely every day until he treats us with the manners due to men of property.'

As they neared Ali's door, the two saw the flickering of a fire through the cracks and heard voices coming from inside the hut. They were afraid to go in— covered with dust and bleeding—without first seeing how the land lay. They put their ears to the door and listened.

'I fear only one thing,' Badfish was saying. 'We ourselves are four grown men and, though we are not accustomed to much money, we are old enough to have perceived the folly of others. If each of us follows the rules of business with the *tinga-tinga* boat we will not perceive loss. My fear is for the two children. They are good children completely, but, since yesterday, I have seen how their heads are getting big. In a little while they will act like people of importance, despise their elders and bring trouble to their Babas by mischief and fighting. I would see great bitterness if this were to be, because I like them much.'

'Do not fear, Old One,' laughed Manowari. 'Their Babas will know how to keep them in order.'

Baba laughed. 'I perceive a road,' he said.

Rajab asked, 'The road of the Kiboko?' (Hippopotamus—and the whip made from its thick hide.)

'No,' answered Baba. 'If they will not behave and do not achieve learning at school they will obtain work in our *tinga-tinga* boat like how?'

There was a laugh at this, and Juma pulled Ali away. They walked in a heavy silence to Juma's door and listened there.

Ali's mother was saying in her soft voice, 'They would have done what without Manowari and the Little Old One—and the Bwana of the lorry?'

'Truly-truly,' said Juma's mother. 'And again, think of the Nakhoda, Haji. I would like much to meet him and give him a blessing, without him they would have been drowned in the sea.'

'They are delaying much in returning from the dance,' said Ali's mother.

'Ah! They are rejoicing, that's all,' was the reply.

Ali and Juma realized that this was a more hospitable door than the other. Juma opened it and they both went in.

'We have finished arriving,' they announced.

Luckily, the little fire at which their mothers were sitting did not show up their dusty, blood-stained condition.

The two women had heard from Manowari and Badfish the story of the boys' adventures. Now, they made a fuss of their sons, gave them strong, sweet tea which they were brewing on the little fire, and soon Ali and Juma were lying in a corner of the small back room, wrapped in blankets.

'Ali, you!' whispered Juma. 'You heard the words of your Baba, about us and the *tinga-tinga* boat?'

'I heard,' Ali answered.

'We will do what?' asked Juma.

'Do work, that's all,' said Ali. 'We wish to be kept out of the *tinga-tinga* boat?'

'We will work—that's all,' sighed Juma. 'I can see no other road.'

.   .   .   .   .

'There is one small question,' muttered Ali. 'Who found this ambari?'

. . . But there was no answer.